THE WORMDIGGER'S DAUGHTER

For Molly and Frank, and their children

JOHN FARRELL

THE WORMDIGGER'S DAUGHTER

MERCIER PRESS
WHAT YOU NEED TO READ

MERCIER PRESS
Douglas Village, Cork
www. mercierpress. ie

Trade enquiries to CMD Distribution
55A Spruce Avenue, Stillorgan Industrial Park,
Blackrock, County Dublin

ISBN: 978 1 85635 574 2

10 9 8 7 6 5 4 3 2 1

Cover illustration detail from Francis Danby's *Disappointed Love*

A CIP record for this title is available from the British Library

 Mercier Press receives financial assistance from the
Arts Council/An Chomhairle Ealaíon

Printed and bound in the UK

❋ Prologue, 2008 ❋

My name is Pat. I come from the north-east side of Dublin – a place where in the past there were big estates and a large farming community. People who worked on the farms and the big estates would come and go, and they lived in little lodges and houses off the estates. The Big House people mockingly called these houses the 'wormdigger's castles'. They called them that because they looked down on the people who worked in the fields – digging the potatoes and ploughing. As far as the landlords were concerned, the estate houses where the workers lived were 'castles' compared to the cabins their families had been born in. It was easy in those days to mock the workers; there were no unions and no other jobs to go to either.

This story began in the mid-1920s when the country was still confused by the things that were happening: independence, the Free State, and the IRA still on the run as if the British were still in charge. But all that made no difference to Molly and Frank. They still worked and did what they were told – at least that is until Molly overheard a conversation that sent a chill through her heart and changed everything for her and her family.

By the time I met Molly and Frank in the early 1950s they must have known somehow that I was their only chance to tell their story. Telling it was a kind of compulsion for them like it is for me now. It has been a great burden on me for the past five decades. It was left with me and I promised to pass it on and that's why I'm telling it now.

This is a true story. There are no big words in it, because no big words would explain some of the things that happened. The people who told it to me didn't use very many big words. Molly and Frank Maguire were their names and Angel was their daughter. Their three young boys had all died of consumption. These were hard times, and they produced strong people.

☀ *Chapter 1* ☀

One night, walking home to my mother's house, I came across a woman and man sitting on the roadside. At first sight I thought they were Travelling folk as they had a little tent set behind the ditch and a small fire made. It was a freezing-cold night. I said 'hello' as I walked by, intending to pass on. But they asked me to stop and sit with them for a while. I really wanted to walk on and not get involved with them, but something in their eyes made me stop. They told me their names were Molly and Frank. They both had a very sad look about them. They asked if I had a fag on me and I did, though my parents didn't know I smoked. So I gave them one each and we all lit up. After a few pleasantries about the weather Molly turned suddenly as if an idea had just struck her.

'Tell him the story,' said Molly.

'I can't,' said Frank.

'Well, I will.' Molly smiled a quiet half-smile at me, a determined look in her blue eyes. She began to tell me a tale that was to stay with me for the rest of my life. Until now I have kept it to myself, often going over it in my own mind again and again. Now I am ready to tell it to you and the rest of the world, just as I promised Molly and Frank I would.

'My children's names were Frank, Peter, Jim and the girl, we called her Angel Marie,' said Molly. 'I know it's a funny name but it's what Frank said when she was born. He came into the house and he says, "God sent us a little angel."

'When we went to get her christened the priest said, "Where did you get a name like that? Sure that's not a name!"

'"Well, she is an angel," I said. "It's Angel Marie and that's the name we'd like her to have. She is our little angel."

'They were all happy children. They had very little but they were very happy and we loved them. That's the way life is: today you're happy and tomorrow you're not.'

Frank turned round and I saw a flicker in his eyes and wasn't sure if it was a trick of the light or a tear. Molly took a box out of her pocket. She opened it up and took out five homemade flowers like those the tinkers used to make.

'We can't get up to the graveyard. We're not able to walk that distance. We thought we could but we can't. Would you put these flowers on my children's graves?'

I looked at her, surprised at this strange request.

'How would I find the graves?' I asked.

'It'll be simple. You go up into the graveyard, you go through the gate and walk along the path. Go to the left when you come to the headstones and walk right round the graveyard to a ditch. You'll see an iron cross and you'll see Maguire written on it. But their names are not on it, only initials. There's F, P and J marked out on the steel cross. Leave the flowers and tell them that we love them and hope to see them in the near future. We aren't able to stand over the grave at the moment because of the way we feel, and if you do that for us we'll pray for you and you can come back tomorrow night and tell us how you got on because we want to tell you our story. We want nothing off anyone, we just want this little job done and maybe we'll be in better form tomorrow night so we can finish telling you everything.'

I took the flowers from Molly and I put them under my coat. 'Goodnight,' I said, and headed for home. I hid the flowers in the shed that night so that no one would see me with them and ask me what I was up to.

The next morning I got up very tired because I hadn't slept. I got the flowers and put them in a little bag and went off up to the graveyard. As I walked around, I saw a little steel cross not too far from the ditch. It was between the footpath and the ditch and *looked very strange to me, like something you'd find on a pauper's grave. I went over and rubbed it with my fingers and I saw the initials F, P and J. I put the flowers down and I said what Molly had asked me to say – that she and Frank loved their children and hoped to see them in the near future. I said a couple of prayers too, I remember, and went off, walking down the pathway. It struck me when I was at the end of the graveyard that there was a name missing from the iron cross – the girl's.*

As I went about my work that morning it was on my mind. At that time I had a job in a shop as a messenger boy, and it was on my mind all day. There was something wrong with the story. If there were four children why were there not four names on the cross – four initials, at least? All day I was thinking and didn't know what to make of it. I thought they were telling me lies about the whole thing and that I'd been made a fool of by going up in the first place.

I couldn't wait for that night to come, to go back and find out. I was going to let them talk first and then I was going to ask why the little girl's initials weren't put on the iron cross. So, when I finished work, I went home and had my tea and I got out a few old coats that were in our shed – they were huntsmen's coats that my father had been given and they were really heavy. I put them into a bag and I went down the road. Molly and Frank were there sitting round the fire.

'How did you get on?' asked Molly.

'Fairly well,' I replied. 'I got that job done this morning. I told

them what you told me to tell them and I left the flowers there. Here,' I added, 'these are a few coats. They'll keep you warm at night and keep out some of the cold.'

'Thank you,' said Molly 'that's very kind.'

We sat down again and Molly made the tea.

'We can't thank you enough for putting the flowers on the grave,' said Molly. Then, out of the blue, Frank turned round and said to Molly, 'Why don't you tell the boy the truth and not wait any longer? Because if you don't tell him the truth, no one will ever know what happened to us.'

'Oh,' she exclaimed, looking straight into my eyes. 'Maybe the boy wouldn't want to hear the whole story?'

'I want you to explain something to me,' I interrupted. 'When I looked at the iron cross this morning and saw the initials, I noticed the girl's initials are not there.'

'My three boys all died within a couple of years of each other.' Molly's eyes were lost in the distance. 'The TB was like that. Lots of children died of it. And the dispensary did nothing for them ...' There was a touch of bitterness in her voice.

Frank, looking at her, put out his hand. 'Easy Molly,' he said, almost in a whisper. There was silence between us all for a while and then Molly looked back at him.

Frank turned to me then and said, 'We're going to come clean about that now. I hope you're willing to listen.'

✳ *Chapter 2* ✳

'When the boys died I was left with Angel,' said Molly. 'When Frank would come home from work at night, I'd have to go up to the Big House and scrub and wash and iron.

'Every bit of dirty work that was there, I'd have to do it. I'd come back to my place at about twelve, maybe one o'clock in the morning, and when I'd get back, Frank would be asleep on the chair because he'd never go to bed while I'd be at work.

'At that time there were big parties up in the house and everything was a celebration. But you weren't allowed to bring any of the food back from the house, all the meat would have to be given to the dogs. The cook would make sure that no one took anything with them. The most trusted people on the estate at that time were the cook, the butler and the land steward. They were as bossy as the bosses themselves, they had the power and they told us what to do and anything that was said about the boss would be carried back immediately to him and you wouldn't know what might happen. They would sack you or do something wrong on you.

'And you weren't supposed to mention anything that went on in the Big House. I'd be clearing the tables and there was clergy there of all dimensions, Protestant ministers, doctors, solicitors, lords and ladies of all description and they had their own way of going on and their own way of enjoying themselves. I don't like saying it to you. It's not nice to hear.'

'Well, I'm fairly open-minded, Molly,' I reassured her. 'You tell me everything. I don't mind, nothing is going to shock me.'

'The only thing that ever shocked me was the loss of my family,' said Molly. 'We'd want to be dead before you told anyone our story. They're still looking for us — the big-estate people and the peelers. You call them guards now. We left the estate in the dead of night and we could never go back.'

'So tell me what you want to tell me. Someday I might be able to bring the truth out in the open for everyone to hear,' I said, for I knew I was a dab hand with a story myself. At home my Mam

and Dad always put me up to tell stories, so an account from people like these would be a great boon for me.

'We'll not travel any more now; I don't think we'll be able. I think that death is near at hand but we'll tell you as much as we can about what happened.'

I'd work as I told you. I'd work in the night-time after Frank came home. During the day I'd open the gates for the people coming on their horses and carriages. Angel would come out and help me; little Angel was a big girl for her age. She was tall and had long blonde hair that blew wildly in the wind when she was out playing. She was a beautiful child. She had such big blue eyes and freckles on her nose. And she was a real busybody, a real chatterbox.

Molly smiled to herself at the memory and paused, thinking before continuing. I was already getting interested in what she was telling me. The big estate and the people in it were still there and I lived on the edge of it myself, even though I didn't know anyone there. Molly continued:

One day two horsemen came up, two gentlemen we used to call them. I was hanging out clothes and Angel was opening the gates for them. I just came up from behind the big pillar that the gates used to hang on. They stopped the horses and said, 'Hello, little girl. What's your name?'

'I'm Angel,' she answered them, and they laughed.

One of the men put his hand in his pocket and took out half a crown, two and sixpence at that time, and gave it to her. He says to the other horseman, 'That one, that's mine. That's mine as soon as she's another year older. The wormdigger's daughter. It's something to look forward to.'

'You're a very lucky man,' said the other.

'I know,' the first replied. 'The Master is giving her to me. He's sending her up to my kitchens in another year, and by the look of her in a few months would be more like it, so I'll have a chat to him about it.'

Well, I was there behind the gate. I got weak in the knees because I knew what he meant and what they were going to do. We had no choice in the matter, because that happened in the Big Houses. When they ran out of women they'd always have the maids to look after them, because maids had no choice – only leave or do what they're told.

Angel closed the gates after the horsemen and I brought her in. 'Mammy,' says she, 'what do they mean?'

'Ah, don't mind them,' I says, 'that's the way men talk you know.'

'I don't want to leave you, Mam, because you've only me left.'

I couldn't hold back the tears.

'Why are you crying, Mam?'

'Ah nothing,' says I. 'I miss the boys.'

'And so do I, Mam,' said Angel. 'I've no one to play with and I don't know what to do with myself. You're not allowed to play with the boys. There is a girl in the Big House belonging to Master Edwards but he won't let her play with me or walk around with me.'

Angel was a clever girl. She could read and write, but they never knew that. Frank Junior used to teach her after he learned behind the furniture sheds. The master's boy, Master Edwards Junior, was a very nice boy and he used to teach Frank Junior how to read and write and gave him books. But the books had to be hidden in case anyone would see them.

That night, when Frank came in from work, he was very tired. 'Don't go to bed yet, I want to talk to you when I come down from the Big House,' I said.

'All right, I'll stay up,' he said.

When I came back it was half-one in the morning. There had been a big hunt ball on and they were all drunk and enjoying themselves. I was told that I would have to come up early in the morning, and not to be disturbing them, to do the floors and things before the master would get up.

'How did you get on?' asked Frank.

So I told Frank what had gone on at the gate that day. He looked at me and I could see his eyes changing. He just stared and never spoke for about ten minutes.

'My God, what else is going to happen to us? I'll have to do something about this but it will have to be done properly and it'll have to be done in a way that no one notices anything. We'll leave here someday. That someday can't be soon enough for me because if anyone touches my little Angel, I'll be in jail over them,' he said.

Frank and I went to bed, but neither of us slept that night, just thinking about what was happening. Frank went to work the next morning and the master called him over and said, 'Maguire, I want you to clean out that big shed. There's an old four-wheel cart there – you can bring it home and use it for firewood – and there's a small trap there; you can take that away and burn it as well.' So Frank did what he was told. He was a handy man doing everything and was made run around the estate like he was a dog.

'And by the way, Maguire,' said the master, 'that horse we bought last year nearly bit one of my children. I'm going to get the vet to put him down and send him over there to use as meat for the hounds.'

'Master Edwards, I'd like that horse to go down to where the garden is, I haven't time to do the garden in the lodge and I could bring him down and let him eat the grass there,' said Frank.

'Well you can bring him down if you want, Maguire,' said the master. 'If he bites your child that's your business, as long as he doesn't bite mine. I don't want him out on the estate.'

Frank thanked him and brought the horse, the cart and the little pony trap back to the house. The horse was very mild mannered with Frank. The master had done something to the horse that he didn't like. Frank always said that animals knew evil and that's why the horse was rough with the master and his family.

After that Frank didn't talk much. He would be out in the shed all night. He would lock the shed in the daytime and I didn't know what he was at. I thought he was going off me and didn't want anything to do with me because the boys were dead and there was no love left in our bodies. But I missed his company. I often asked him what he was doing out in the shed and he'd say, 'I'm just tinkering around keeping myself busy.'

'We don't get much time for talking now, Frank,' I would say, and he'd say, 'No, the talk has gone out of me, but it's not your fault and it's not anyone's fault.'

So Frank continued his work and came home in the evening and had something small to eat. I'd wash up and then go to the Big House and this continued for months.

One day I was in the lodge and the parish priest came round. I hadn't seen him even when the children died, because it was hard to get him. He said, 'You're better off without children that are delicate; they're not much good to the master because you have no one to step in if Frank gets sick. You have to have people to keep the master going.' That's what he said.

'Father, the master is well looked after by the staff and by whoever he is dealing with in business but we're not being looked after,' I said.

'A big strong woman like you. You should have another heap of children and then make sure that the master's not short of staff, because that's what keeps these big estates going,' said the priest.

'I've no interest in the estate, or the master, or his place,' I replied.

'You're a very ungrateful woman and I hope you're not going through marital acts without thinking about having children because it's a mortal sin and you shouldn't be doing that if you don't think about having children. You should have more children. There's nothing wrong with you so you should have more children,' he said.

'You mention love there, Father. The love is gone out of our bodies after the loss of our family and everything, and you come to me and tell me that I should be having more children to make sure that the master and people like him has plenty of cheap labour?'

'You're a very ungrateful woman, and you'll go to hell for this way you're talking and thinking,' he retorted.

'Father, I *am* in hell and we've been in hell from the first day we ever put our foot into this place.'

'After the master put a roof over your head and food in your stomachs, and this is the way you pay him back!' said the priest.

I was angry.

'I'm sorry Father, but this is the end of the conversation. I saw you up at the ball the other night, you and all the other big people from around enjoying yourselves, and us coming home and lying in squalor and dampness, and no one cares. No one even asked about how we felt about our children dying. They wouldn't even come to the funeral and they didn't give us nearly enough time to bury them.'

He went out the door and he banged it after him.

The next morning Frank was crossing the yard and Master Edwards said, 'Come here, Maguire, I want to talk to you. What sort of a wife is that you have? She's a very ungrateful person. I've a good mind to throw you all out on the road and end your contract if she doesn't come up here and apologise.'

'I'm sorry, Master Edwards,' said Frank, 'I don't know anything about this.'

'Oh! Does she keep secrets from you as well?' said the master.

So Frank looked at him and said, 'Well, we haven't been getting on since the children died and maybe there's something wrong with her.'

'There is nothing wrong with her that a good belt with a stick wouldn't cure. She's not to insult me or my family or my friends. She mentioned the hunt ball, and the carry-on at it, and that they didn't care about her or her children or anything. Well, I want her up here to apologise or else you'll go,' thundered the master.

Frank came home that night and said, 'Molly, you did an awful wrong thing.'

'What did I do?' I asked.

'You went on to the priest about how you felt and the injustices done on us. I know it's true, Molly, but you don't want to be put out on the road, not just yet. For God's sake, will you go up and apologise to him this morning and tell him you didn't know what you were talking about, that with the loss of the children and all that, you was losing the head a bit.'

'That's an awful request, Frank. I'd do anything for you but that's an awful request,' I said.

'Molly, trust me, I'll make it good, I'll do my best to rectify it, but for now, will you go up and apologise?'

'All right, I'll go up and do it.'

As I walked up the avenue I met the master coming down and he stopped his pony. 'Now, Maguire, you had enough to say about me to the parish priest and what explanation are you going to give me?'

'Well, master,' I said, 'I did not know what I was saying. I lost the children and I think I'm going a bit funny in the head but I'm very sorry and I hope you accept my apology and it won't happen ever again.'

'I'll take that for now and if you see the parish priest

apologise to him too about what you said or what you saw. What did you see anyway, Molly?'

'I saw nothing, Master Edwards, nothing,' I said.

'That's the way to be and that's the way to survive here,' he went on. 'Be seeing nothing and saying nothing. You're only peasants and I'm keeping a roof over your heads and I make the rules round here, not you. If I want your daughter up here to work or anything like that I can demand her and I can demand her to stay. And you have no choice but to do that or get out.'

'Will you accept my apology, Master Edwards?' I asked.

'I will. Now, go off about your business and keep your mouth shut.'

I went on up to the house and finished my cleaning and scrubbed the slabs on the floor.

'I hear you're going around bad-mouthing Lord Edwards,' said the cook.

'I didn't know what I was saying,' I replied.

'If I hear anything again I'll sack you. You see nothing in here. We're the people you have to work for; you're not working with us, you're working *for* us. So keep your mouth shut and go on about your business.'

I finished work and went home. I rapped on the shed door and Frank called out, 'I'll be there in a minute.' After about a half an hour, Frank locked the shed and came in.

'How did you get on?' he asked.

'I apologised and I done what you asked me. But it went to my heart apologising to him. He said he owns us and he can say and do what he wishes and what he pleases with us, to our daughter or to anyone else who is under his roof. So what do you think of that, Frank?'

'Molly, 'tis shocking an' all but what can I do? I have asked you to leave it with me and let me sort it out. I'm the man of the house and I've lost my children the same as you did. I'll sort it. I brought you to this place and I'll take you from it, but no one is going to know when, where or how. I hope you realise what I'm trying to do. And I'm not going off you,' he went on. 'I still love you, but I've a lot to do, and I'm tired. Don't ask me about moving or what to do or anything. Let me think. Maybe I'm not educated and can't read or write, but I can think and I'll be able to manage. I got us into this and I'll get us out of it.'

✳ *Chapter 3* ✳

*T*wo days later, the doorbell rang and who was outside only the doctor. He had his pony and trap as well and I let him in the gate and he stopped and got off the trap.

'I hear you're not very happy with the way I dealt with your children,' he said.

'You must know the way I feel about the loss of my children. I am left with only one daughter. She misses her brothers so much and that leaves it hard on me. Maybe I said too much?' I replied.

'You're a lucky woman for anyone like me to put my hands on you,' said the doctor. 'You're very ungrateful. I'm too busy with the master's children not being well and with the people who pay me. I haven't much time for people like you. I get paid for my work and you are looking for something for nothing. It's the master who looks after me if I do anything for his staff. We have our families to rear and put them through college and we can't depend on the likes of you penny-a-week people.'

'I hope doctor, that the day will never come that you'll have to live like me, but we have to put up with what we get,' I said.

'We rear our own families and educate them. It's up to everyone to look after themselves in this life,' he replied.

'If you could call it a life,' I said.

'This is the life you chose and this is what you get. You work until you're not able and then you go into the poorhouse and spend the rest of your days there. I have my way of life and the people who give it to me are the people I look after,' he said.

I wished him the best of luck because I didn't want him going up and saying anything to Master Edwards, but my blood was boiling when I thought of what he was saying to me. I went into the house and was in that much of a rage I cried my eyes out.

When Frank came back in the evening I told him everything the doctor had said.

Frank went silent. He never opened his mouth, just stared at me.

'Frank, I said nothing to him.'

'They're all the one here. They tell each other everything because they're all looking after themselves and their interests. I know that,' said Frank.

I told Frank I wouldn't be able to stick it much longer.

'Maybe you won't have to. Just carry on what you're doing and keep quiet and we'll just survive some way.'

'Angel will be twelve in another few weeks,' I reminded him, 'and they'll be looking for her to get out of school so you know the score. She'll have to go to work above or with one of the master's friends.'

'He promised one of them that he'd get him a nice good-looking maid and they help each other out like that, Molly,' said Frank. 'I'll do my best to make sure she won't leave our sight. It's all getting very difficult for me.'

Things went back to normal for a while. Frank went to work in the morning and was back in the evening and I went to scrub the floors, even though I didn't get paid for it – it was part of the rent for the lodge we were in. I often had to keep Angel home from school to open the gates during the day, especially if I had to go to town to get a few things.

Time went on. Frank was getting more distant from me. There was no contact between the two of us at all. We would just say a few words to each other and he would go on out into his shed and I was always thinking to myself what the hell is he doing in there? Is he sitting in there just not to be with me?

The shed came with our lodge. A lot of the machinery from the estate that had been kept there was taken up to another shed behind the Big House so our shed was now empty. I wondered what Frank was doing in an empty shed.

Even Angel felt a bit distant from him. But he had a lot on his mind and so had I. It disrupted our whole lives; we were falling apart. Frank was still on the job and he'd walk the horse around. I often asked myself what business he had with the horse. He'd be down with the blacksmith a lot too. He would bring the horses down to get them shod.

Frank and the blacksmith were great friends. If Frank had a few free hours he'd go down and dig the garden for the blacksmith. It was the blacksmith that made the cross for us for the boy's grave and it was the best of steel he put into it. He used to show Frank how to shoe horses.

'Never let them see you doing anything for me or helping me out shoeing horses,' the blacksmith said, 'or they'll take the horses off me and destroy my business. You're very welcome to come down any time to me and I'll show you how to shoe horses and bend steel.'

The blacksmith had great sympathy for us because he had lost a child too and he understood the pain we were going through.

One day Angel said to me, 'Why have you and Dad no brothers or sisters?'

'I don't know, Angel,' I said. 'There was only one in your dad's family and only one in mine.'

'It must have been very lonesome without any brothers or sisters,' said Angel.

'I don't know about that. I was used to having no brothers or sisters and I suppose your Dad was the same. We knew each other because we lived beside each other. Frank's dad died and then my father died young. When my mother died too we said we'd get married and that we'd have lots of children to make up for the life we'd had. But that wasn't to be. We've just ended up with one child. The others all dead. But we're delighted with you and we love you.'

'I know that, Mam,' she said. 'But I often wondered was there a reason that the two of you met and neither you nor Dad having a brother or sister.'

I just said to her, 'Well, that's the way life goes.'

One day Frank came back with the horse and cart from the estate. He was delivering some of the timber around to the estate houses – everyone was given their share of timber, which was very small, every week. You were not allowed to cut the estate timber at night-time or anything. You'd be given enough timber to keep you going for the week. Frank came out. He'd thrown off the timber he had on the cart and he'd an old horse harness.

'Molly,' he asked me, 'would you bring in that harness? I want to repair it and polish it up because I might be able to sell it off unbeknownst to the boss. He told me to dump it. So would you put the harness in one of the rooms? I'll get you to stitch it some night, and you can put a bit of new lining on the horse's collars and the saddles.'

I looked at Frank and laughed and said, 'What are you going to do? Sure that's junk!'

'No it's not,' said Frank. 'That's good stuff. There's the best of leather in that. We'll stitch it up, we'll make it good. We'll get a few pound for it maybe when I have it fixed.'

So I'd help him some of the nights. He'd come in early enough from the shed. We were stitching the harness and we were beginning to talk a little more than we had. But it was an awful thing to bring into the house. You could smell the horse sweat off it.

'Oh,' he said. 'That's no harm! I'm with horses every day of the week so it don't smell that bad to me.'

And we were laughing about it. Even Angel said the next day, 'You and Daddy were laughing last night.'

'Oh, we were! We were just laughing about things we seen years ago.'

I didn't tell her that he'd brought in the harness, in case she'd let it slip at school that we were fixing it up to sell it. She was happy too to hear us talking. For a week or so, we were stitching and fixing and polishing, and it looked lovely. Then we left it in the room and covered it with an old blanket so that if anyone was looking in they wouldn't see it.

Nothing else came down from the estate because there was very little left in it that you could sell. That was all done by the land steward – it was up to him what could go and what could stay.

Frank seemed to be happy enough. He was talking a little more. I asked him one day: 'Did you ever think any more about what we're going to do?'

'Oh,' he says, 'I think of it regularly, Molly. There's not a day or a night that I don't think of what to do, but I have to be very sensible about how I do it.'

I said to him, 'Frank – look, don't do anything foolish and don't get yourself into trouble or anything.'

He stared back at me. 'Molly,' he said, 'I never did anything foolish in my life.'

'Oh you did, Frank. You married me!'

And the laughing started again. But he had a gleam in his eye and I didn't like it. I didn't know what he was up to and I was getting more curious by the day because he couldn't hide things very well. This is why I was so upset by the silence between us because he'd never been like that before. He was always open and loyal. I told him that. He let out a laugh. 'Do you think of me that way, Molly? That I'm a loyal man to you?'

'Oh indeed you are, Frank. Don't be so modest – you are loyal, you're a good man.'

✳ *Chapter 4* ✳

Frank came home one day and said the master's brother in England was not well. He had a big estate in Cambridge. I never was in England so I don't know where it is. And he told me the master'd be going over because a son was at college over there and he was going to help his brother out till he was well enough to do his own work again and look after the estate. The master was taking the land steward with him and they'd be gone for three or four weeks, five at the most. Him and the land steward and the master's wife and young daughter were going over.

'I have a lot more duties to take on,' Frank said. 'I've to do more rounds; I've to do half the land steward's job. But there'll be no one there, only me and a few others to look after the estate whilst they be away. The cook is going on a holiday and they'll all be gone in a week's time so I'll have a load more work to do. It's going to be harder on us again.' He just shrugged his shoulders.

The week went by, ten days or so, and then the master, the land steward, and all went off over to England, to this Cambridge where the big estate was. The cook stayed on for five or six days after that to see that everything was in order, getting out the rations for the staff who were living in and putting someone in charge till she came back. She was the boss in the house and she liked to get things done her way.

After she left, Frank came home and said, 'There's no one above. I'm working away and I'll be back early this evening and you won't have to go up to the Big House to work. You'll be doing kitchen duties. But you won't have to scrub or do anything like that. When I get back tonight I'll tell you what I want you to do.'

So I finished up the jobs I had to do, cooked a meal for the staff, and helped do things around the place. It was very relaxed with the cook gone and no one in the Big House.

At home that night, sitting down, Frank said to me, 'Molly, I want to tell you something. I was going to tell you before now but I want to show you something as well. Come with me. I don't want Angel to know anything about this.'

He brought me outside, he opened the shed and there it

was: the four-wheel cart that he had brought down from the estate. It was all painted, done up with a canopy attached to it. It was like one of the wagons you'd see in a cowboy film. And he had a little trap with a bar coming out of it, or a shaft, to pull behind.

'This is what I was doing in the shed,' he said. 'I was making a wagon for us to go and a place in the wagon for Angel and us to sleep in, and the other trap would be pulled behind and we could put all the utensils or whatever we have into it. And I've a spare wheel there for the wagon and one for the trap. I got that out of the big shed. The harness is for the horse. I've been bringing oats in me pockets for the horse for the last couple of months and building him up. He's a lovely animal and he's going to help us to get away from here.'

'But how are you going to do it, Frank?'

'Just leave it to me,' he said. 'What do you think?'

'I can't believe what I'm looking at,' I said. 'I suppose I'm excited! And a bit frightened too. But it's lovely, just lovely.'

You could stand up in the wagon and there was beds made out of wood and mattresses of straw and we had some stuff in the house – pillows and that – but these mattresses made of straw were clean. A lot of people used to call them 'ticks'. They used to use the chaff from the thresher mills but we packed these ones with straw instead. They weren't too soft, but with a few blankets on them they'd be all right. The two of us were lying in the bed and we laughed.

'This is an adventure we're going on and you're going to enjoy every minute of it – the freedom of the road,' he said. 'I've been speaking to a lot of gypsy people and they gave me directions so, though I can't read or write much, I'll be able to go by these lines on the paper showing places we can pull in and names of farmers on the way.'

'On the way where, Frank?'

'Well, I'll just tell you now. We're going to Cork.'

'But that's nearly two hundred miles away!'

'Well it could be but it doesn't matter. I'll tell you when to get ready. We'll start preparing. Bring down food from that house every night and we'll eat well. Don't let anyone see you. I've enough oats and hay that will do until we get somewhere I can work for a couple of days and feed the horse and stuff like that. We're getting out of here, but I won't tell you when because it's not all ready yet. I'm even getting excited over it myself! I couldn't keep it a secret any longer.'

The two of us put our arms around each other and we hugged for about ten minutes with tears falling down from both our eyes. We didn't know whether we were crying for joy or regret for not having left a long time ago.

I said to Frank, 'I wonder would the boys be alive if we had done this before?'

'No,' says Frank. 'Only for Master Edwards going away we'd never get out of here. But I have a plan and I hope it works for Angel's and your sake. You know the consequences.

It's going to be tough. They're going to be looking for us. And they'll accuse us of everything – stealing and crimes of every kind. I can see it all before it starts. This is what we have to think about. I'll put this plan into action soon. It won't be weeks. It'll be days. So gather up whatever you have and get it ready. Get it washed and packed. But don't let anyone know what you're doing. I have to go and bring the horse down to the blacksmith's to get him shod. He gave me a heap of shoes he made for the horse. The blacksmith knows what I'm going to do. So I'll be bringing the horse down to him one of the evenings when it gets dark and when no one can see me going. I know how to change the shoes and how to pare his feet and stuff like that. We'd never get away if the master was here or the land steward. The rest of them's not clever enough to find us out yet. We've a big long weekend coming up and there'll be no one in the house for about three or four days or maybe five days. I'm supposed to be looking after the place for those few days. That's when we'll do it.'

'Frank, that's very risky. What's going to happen?'

'Well,' he said to me, 'I don't know what's going to happen. But there's a woman above in the house and she's undecided whether she's going away or not. She doesn't know what's happening so I'll be talking to her today and I'll find out what she's going to do. It'll be better if she stayed in the house because you wouldn't know what they'll accuse us of taking.'

Frank came back again that evening when he had all his work done and he had his tea and said to me, 'Now, when you're up there, bring food down, eat well, feed Angel well and I'll eat well. The horse will be eating well too for the journey.' So I did that. Every day I came down, I brought something with me, meat out of the fridge – they had plenty of it. You were supposed to give it to the dogs, you weren't supposed to eat it yourself. But we ate it and the dogs put up with bread and milk.

On a Thursday evening Frank came in and he said, 'We're leaving on Friday night. I've everything right. The horse is shod; I have his shoes, enough to last him about six to eight months. I've all my tools packed away. We'll be ready to go Friday night. We'll travel through the night. We'll head for Dublin and from Dublin to Cork. It's going to be hard and it's going to take a long time but we have to go. We can't wait any longer because the woman above is not going away. She's going to stay in the estate house so that'll give us a few days in case anything goes wrong. So be ready.'

Friday came and I had everything ready. I'd packed the wagon and the trap and Frank came and finished it off.

Angel asked, 'What's happening, Dad?'

'We're leaving here,' he says. 'We're leaving now and we're not going to come back here.'

Well, she jumped for joy and we brought her in and showed her the wagon and she thought it was great.

'This is lovely. Where are we going?'

'We're going far away love,' he told her. 'And we're not coming back. We're never going to work on a place like this again because we want you to have a better life.'

Friday night came, and we moved out. It was a winter's night, and dark. We'd two lamps, one on each side of the wagon. They were lamps you had to put candles into. There was no traffic on the road. Those days there was nothing really; you wouldn't meet a cart at that hour of the night or anybody really on the roads. We headed off down and onto a back road and then onto the Dublin road. We travelled all night. Frank stopped anywhere there was water to give the horse a drink and a rest and at ten o'clock the next morning we arrived in Dublin city. There were carts everywhere and ponies and traps and old-fashioned carriages. Angel was amazed at what she saw. We went all along the Liffey and then headed for the Cork road.

Frank says, 'We can't stay around here tonight. We'll need to get to some farm or some camp where we can pull in. If we pull in at a camp, they won't know where the cart came from or anything like that. I'll have to grow a beard and there'll have to be something done about Angel's hair and yours. You'll have to get a shawl and we'll have to act as if we're Travelling people.'

On the Cork road we went about eight miles or so further on and came to this little lay-by where there were Travellers' wagons. We pulled in. One of the Travellers said, 'That's a fine cart,' he said. 'That's the best I've seen.'

Frank nodded. 'It's a long story.'

'If you don't want to be seen around here,' the Traveller said, 'you better pull well in there so they won't see your wagon. There's space there. You can put the horse in for the night along with ours and there won't be any bother.'

We sat talking there for ages with him and then we said, 'It's time to go to bed.'

'Well, you'll meet someone here in the morning that'll help you out. You're not Travellers but I know you're running from something. We might be able to help you do whatever you want to do.'

The next morning we got up and the Travellers had a big fire lit and there was tea and bread and everything you could mention. They seemed to have plenty of food and we'd a bit of food stored up ourselves. They shared what they had with us and we shared what we had with them. We told them what had happened and what we wanted. We told them that they'd be looking for us and asked them what was the best thing we could do. Our Traveller friend said to just stay there for a couple of days and we might hear from other Travellers if there was anyone looking for us.

'I don't think there'll be anyone looking for us for at least two weeks,' Frank told him. 'How long do you think it will be before we get near Cork?'

'Well,' said the Traveller, 'you could do it fast but you don't want to kill your animal. They can only do so much a day before they have to pull in. There's the odd farmer on that road who'll give you some work. Are you any way handy?'

Says Frank, 'You see what I've done on the wagon.'

'You'll get the odd bit of work. It'll keep you going. It'll keep you in food. The farmers who'll give you the work, they haven't much money. But they'd give you plenty of food and look after your horse and your child and your wife.'

The next day we hit the road again and took it nice and easy. We rested the horse every now and then, and anywhere we found a river we'd give him a wash down and let him out to run around the field. You'd think the horse knew what we were doing. Angel would go up to him and he'd be rubbing his nose against her. She called him Bobby, and he nearly knew his name. She loved that horse. We went on for miles till we came to this farmer's yard. Frank went up and asked him had he any work.

'I have plenty,' he said, 'but I haven't any money.'

'If you look after my horse and wife and child there, that'll do me nicely and you can give me a couple of shillings when I'm going,' Frank offered.

'I want the sheds fixed up and a few things done round the place. Are you a handy man?'

'I am,' Frank told him. 'I'll do anything you want me to do if you look after us.'

So we pulled into his yard and kept our wagon well out of sight and did the work for him. He fed us well and looked after us. He had a shed for workmen coming and going and at least we had a bed. I helped the lady in the house and she was very nice. She had children herself. I told her our story and what was happening and the woman was sorry for us.

'The day is going to come,' she said, 'when this will stop and won't happen to people any more. They're very cruel. I'll help you the best I can and that's all we can do. We haven't got much money. We're rearing a family ourselves on a small farm and …'

'Oh, I understand,' I says to her.

Frank and the farmer got on well together and had a lot of great talks.

'You're not a Traveller, Frank?' the farmer asked him one day. So Frank told him what had happened to us. 'I'd love to look after you and keep you here but the police come round an odd time to see if I've a dog licence or if the cattle break into another man's field or something. It'd be very dicey because they'd cop on about who you are. That child you have, she's very noticeable, she's a very good-looking girl. You'll have to do something about that because the first thing they're going to notice is that child – she stands out. You'll have to do something to disguise her.'

The farmer was a straight-talking man.

Frank asked me, 'Molly, what are we going to do about Angel? We'll have to cut her hair and make her look like a boy and put a cap and trousers on her.'

'We'll have to talk to her,' I told him. It was breaking my heart even to think of cutting her hair and making a boy out of her but the farmer's wife offered to do it. So we called Angel and told her.

'You'll have to look like a boy because you're going to be noticed if you stay the way you are.'

'Well, Mam,' she said, 'if we're in danger, my hair and the fact that I'm a girl doesn't matter. Do whatever you need to do. I don't want to go back to that estate again.'

The farmer's wife took Angel in and cut her hair, tied it in a ribbon and put it in a box. I said, 'Angel, it's here in a box behind me. I'll show it to you one day.'

It broke my heart but it had to be done. We dressed her up as a boy and called her Patrick. We went on the road a couple of days later. We went from village to town and from town to village. The farmer had given us a couple of addresses where, if we mentioned his name, they'd give us a bit of work and a bit of food. And that's how we went on.

✳ *Chapter 5* ✳

*W*e travelled and travelled. People were very nice to us and they understood our case. Each farmer gave us a letter to bring to the next farmer so their address and all would be on it. But one day we stopped in this village – this was a good few weeks after we'd set out – and Angel saw a poster outside a post office. It said they were looking for a Maguire family who had robbed the estate, and robbed the horse and other property belonging to the estate. It said they broke their contract and that there was a reward of ten pound for information about their whereabouts. Ten pound was a fortune at that time.

We had to leave that village that day. But they were

looking for a man and a woman and a blonde girl and we didn't fit that description. Frank had let a beard grow and I had cut my hair short and wore a shawl, and Angel was disguised as a boy. So we didn't match the poster. Worst of all was the reward money. You couldn't trust anyone because things were very bad and ten pound was an awful sight of money. We just decided to keep going – and to keep out of the villages and towns. Any place we thought we might be stopped, we'd go through at night and if there were Travellers on the road we'd join in with them. That was the safest thing to do.

We went past a police station one day and saw the poster again, with descriptions of a girl with long blonde hair. The reward had gone up to twenty pound. We were getting more afraid by the day – what we were accused of had never happened. We took nothing but they wanted to get us because they were afraid we'd tell what was going on in the Big Houses with the staff and young girls and all that.

We were blessed in a way because Angel could read and write. If I went into the village I'd bring her – him, for she looked like a boy at this stage. Frank would do the same – they'd go off like a man and his son just walking round to do a bit of shopping. We couldn't be seen together, the three of us. 'Twas very hurtful to hear what they were saying about us. That's why we're telling you what happened so it'll never happen to anyone again. We were treated like animals. Treated terrible and ran down, made little of, we were nobody. That's the way we felt with every poster we saw. They made us criminals and put us on the run.

We kept going for another couple of weeks and we came within ten mile of Cork. We got a job with a farmer there and Frank worked and I did the scrubbing and the washing for them. They were very good to us.

The farmer at the next big farm that we pulled into said, 'Will you do a few jobs for me? I'll give you a few pound when all the work is done. Stay with me till then. I want the inside and the outside of the house fixed up.'

Frank worked hard there for a few weeks and I worked hard in the house. Angel used to come and help out and they were saying, 'That's a lovely boy.' So we explained to the farmer and his wife that she was a girl and we told them about the big estate and why we left. They understood straight away because at that time there were people who knew the kind of things that happened on estates – they had meetings and were called the Brotherhood – and lots of these farmers on outlying farms seemed to be in that organisation. We were given a letter to bring to another farmer within five miles of Cork. When we were going on the road again to do the last ten miles, he gave us ten pounds in shillings. It was a bag of silver.

'I didn't give you a note because they'd wonder where you got it. So you can have your shillings.'

We were over the moon. It was a great lot of money and we thanked him and headed off on the last few miles. Within five miles of Cork, we delivered our letter to the next farmer and we stopped there for nearly a fortnight. But Frank wanted to go and find a place for us where he could pull the wagon in and hide it. The farmer knew someone and sent Frank to him with a letter. So Frank went off and met this farmer and got a welcome into his house.

'Bring your wagon down here. I've a small house down in the farm you can have for as long as you want. I'll look after you. You're a good man and we'll get on fine.'

Frank came back delighted. He brought another letter back with him too. We didn't know what all the letters were about, or what was going on, but the next day we headed down the last five miles. We pulled into the farmyard and everything was big – big sheds and a big yard and a big farmhouse. The farmer, Pearse, and his wife, Florence, were very nice. We knew their names but we never used them because we worked for them – it just wouldn't have been right. The only problem we had was with Angel. We didn't want her to mix with other children because we didn't want anyone to find out she was a girl. The boys from the neighbouring farms used to come round asking, 'Can Patrick come out to kick football? Is he coming out to play?' I'd have to say he had a bad chest and poor Angel would be dumbfounded. She didn't know what to say or what to do.

Our future depended on Angel not being recognised because the posters were everywhere.

We settled in and started to work on the farm. We moved into the house and we had beds and everything we wanted. We even had a dresser for delft.

Then the farmer says, 'I'd like to buy that cart off you. It's a fine wagon and I could bring in my hay and that in it.'

Frank agreed, and the farmer said, 'I'll take the horse if you're not going to need him any more. I'll give you a few pounds for the lot. Even the trap is a nice thing. I could use that myself or you could use it. I've a pony there and with the trap you could go in and out of town. You can have the pony as long as you want. I'll keep the horse to do the work on the farm.'

So Frank and the farmer made a deal and we had a trap to go in and out of the town – we wouldn't want to be seen walking. Saturday we'd have a half-day and Sunday we had off. We used to go to Mass and down to the harbour and watch the ships go in and out. It was lovely. We dreamed about getting on a ship to America. I'd heard so much about America, about the 'land of dreams'. But we didn't know what to do or how to go about anything. Every weekend we'd bring Angel to watch the ships. You could see her eyes light up when she'd see the people getting off and on the ships. She'd always ask, 'Can we not go, Mammy, go with them people to America? I read about America in school and it's a great place to get rich.'

We used to take her to watch the ships come and go. We could look at boats coming in and out but we couldn't get on them for we hadn't the right papers and no way of getting them. One day we made a few enquiries and were told that we would need identification, and we said we'd get that in order and get back to them. But we knew this was another dream to be shattered because we no longer had an identity.

Angel was getting very wise and was developing into a young woman so we had to start binding her chest to keep it from showing. She took after Frank, and was tall for a girl. It was getting harder and harder to keep her safe.

✳ *Chapter 6* ✳

We went home that evening and talked a lot about what our next plan might be. What could we do to try and get a new life for ourselves and Angel? She was the reason we were there and our only reason for living. We had to show her that we were strong and determined to do something for ourselves after all that had happened to us. But as the weeks went on and the months went by nothing changed. We often went back to the port to watch the boats come in and go out and the people getting off and on. Some were happy; a lot were sad. We often wondered did they really know how bad it was when you couldn't go on the boat at all, when you knew that you were stuck and you had someone very young with their future in front of them and you were losing a battle that you had not started. To try to keep a brave face on all the time was an awful strain. Especially when you were trying to hide it from a little girl with her eyes set on the world and her dreams. Hope followed us like a disease but there was no let-up, no sign of an opening we could take. But we were definitely not going back – we were going forward.

A whole lot of people asked us why we didn't go to England. But our thinking was that the big landlords and their solicitors and barristers were as much in touch with London and England and the English police as they were in Meath. They wouldn't be long catching up with us there, and we'd be lost. I belonged to no country or had no country to belong to. But I wanted my daughter to have a country to belong to and people to belong to.

We had no immediate relatives, so if anything happened to us Angel would be on her own. I don't think she would have been able to cope with that. We had to wait for something to happen. We didn't want Angel to go back. We didn't want her interfered with by thugs and people that didn't care about us peasant people, people that only wanted their money's worth out of us. I don't want to have to say it – you're only a young chap listening to me – but they all wanted their way with the nice young women that worked on the estates. And nine times out of ten, they got it. This is what we were facing. That is what we were watching. There was no point in putting her into a convent or anywhere like that because she'd be found out and taken and made to work for these people.

We were better off on the road along with the Travelling people. At least they had morals among themselves. They loved their children and weren't interfering with them in any way. But in the big society, they didn't care who you were or what you were. They'd get what they wanted and that was all there was to it.

'I was always afraid I might never be able to tell my story, Pat. We're getting old and don't have much time left so you're a godsend to us, you are. I don't want to come face to face with the people that did these things to us but time will catch up with them soon enough. I believe that we'll all meet up in the one place and I hope there's no reserved place for those who had heaven on earth here. But back at that time what I wanted was Angel secure and me and Frank able to live and die in peace. That's all we wanted, Pat. But let's go back to the story …'

❋ *Chapter 7* ❋

*B*y our second year on the run, the strain on me and Frank was beginning to show, and things were worse for Angel. She would be fourteen her next birthday which was a couple of months away. She was growing up and was sore because we had her all bound up as a boy. She had no life, none whatsoever. There were a few people who wanted to adopt her but we would have had to tell them where she came from and have her birth certificate so we'd answer that she was too old. She was never registered. She was christened but, wherever it was on the day, there was no book to write in her details. I knew that because I went one day for a birth certificate and there was none, so they gave me a note instead with what I told them – the date, time and place. That was another drawback. She had no identification documents. As far as anyone was concerned she didn't exist.

We didn't know what to do about that either. No matter what country you'd be in, you would have to show some sort of papers but we had none. We were homeless, familyless and countryless. We had no origin at all and no papers. We were fugitives on the run. Whether we had papers or not, they would still have their pound of flesh. It was really killing us because we didn't understand it all – the papers you needed for people to call you by your name. We hadn't got them for her. Where our own certificates were I didn't know either. When we were getting married we had to get a letter of freedom. That was easy – the parish priest where we came from just gave it to us and that was all. So there was no way we could do anything about Angel. Unless she and her parents had proper identification, an adoption order wouldn't go through. That is what these small farmers who helped us told us. We had a girl acting as a boy and we had to do something to release her from that terrible ordeal.

We still went to the harbour once in a while to watch the boats come in and out, in and out, in and out. One Sunday this boat arrived from America. When it docked, the people on deck were all clapping. You couldn't believe the excitement there on the quayside. Me and Frank and Angel got as near to the gangway as we could. But there was a barrier so you couldn't get in close. Angel was taller than me and she could see over all the heads what was going on – the hugging and the kissing and the welcoming. Our eyes were glued to the people being welcomed. This could be us, I was saying to myself. This could be me and Angel and my boys coming back to visit Ireland. It was a daydream I had always had.

We walked slowly back up the quays and were sitting on a bench talking about this and that when a man and woman came over to us and asked could we tell them the name of the hotel owned by the Sweeneys in the town.

'We don't know, we're not from this place,' I answered. 'But sure if you ask someone around …'

'Everyone is gone! Somebody was supposed to meet us but we must have missed them. You're Irish so we thought you might know.'

The man spoke very cheerfully. I'd never heard such an accent in all my life. He was the first American I ever spoke to. 'I thought everyone in Ireland knew each other,' he said, smiling.

'Well, we don't,' says Frank, and he half-choked listening to these happy people. He had a sadness in his voice. 'Some of us know some people and more of us probably knows no one at all.'

'Well, that's not what I learned from my father. My grandfather came from this town. He's buried somewhere out in the country there. I never met him but I mean to see their graves. They were very poor – that's why my father went to America. He got a job on a ship and he got off in America and stayed there. The same with my wife here. Her people are from Kerry, and we're going to see their graves as well.' He talked a lot so we walked on a bit with them.

'That's a lovely boy you have there. What age is he?'

'Fourteen next birthday,' I says proudly.

'The young people in America are very forward and they come up to you and talk, but he seems to be very shy.'

'He is a bit shy. He doesn't meet many people,' I said.

But the man seemed to be staring at us. Not at us but through us, and the woman didn't speak for a while. And she seemed to be looking through us too. I don't know what they saw in our faces or what they were thinking. It was unreal the way they kept staring at us and we were getting embarrassed and began shuffling away. They're Americans, I kept telling myself, trying to make myself more comfortable with their attentions.

'Would you like to meet us tomorrow?' the American said suddenly. 'We'd love to hear a bit of local history and have someone to show us around. We could meet up and have some tea or lunch. Whatever you'd like. And I'll gladly pay you for your trouble.' He was looking at Frank. 'You'd be saving me a lot of bother if you could help me out – find out where the graveyard is and a few other things I want to know. Can we meet you back in the square at eleven o'clock tomorrow morning?'

Frank surprised me when he said, 'I will. I'll meet you. In the square tomorrow.'

'Well,' says the American, 'bring your wife and son with you when you come.'

'Oh, I wouldn't like to put that on you,' says Frank.

'Not at all. You bring your wife and your son and we'll have a nice day. You'll show me around and you can help me out. I see there's a pony and trap tied up there. Is it yours?'

'It is,' says Frank.

'Well then. You can take us around for the weekend! We don't know too many here. We're going to meet our cousins. They're supposed to own a hotel here. We've been writing to them for a year. We're off there now. We'll enquire somewhere else where this hotel is.'

So off they walked but they kept glancing back.

I asked Frank, 'What do you think of that?'

'I don't know what to think of them,' he said, 'but I could feel them looking at me.'

'So could I,' I agreed. 'But who are they Frank? What do they want?'

'They're the people you wanted to go over to see – Americans. Isn't that where you want to go? I wonder if all the people are like that in America, looking through you?'

I laughed and Frank laughed and said, 'Well, maybe it's us that was staring at them, at their lovely clothes and the smell of perfume.'

'I don't know, Frank, but maybe you're right. I think I

might have seen something in them that I want for Angel. Imagine her coming back at their age and saying, "My mother and father lived here and suffered at the hands of the rich." This is what I was thinking. More dreams. We're all dreaming and no action, so we are!'

'Molly, that's all we have left. The one thing no one can take from us is our dreams and our thoughts. This is something we're going to live with and die with. Not only our dreams, our little secrets. If anyone today recognised us and handed us over to the police, they wouldn't be long prising our secrets open. I don't know whether we should go tomorrow or not. I don't know what to think, I don't know what to say and I don't know what to do.'

'Maybe you'd go on your own Frank, and bring them round the place.'

'What would I do without you to talk to them, and Angel to take down their names? Sure we'd be lost without each other. The three of us. So if one goes, we all go. And if one stays away, we all stay away.'

We got the big basin bath out and we washed ourselves and got ourselves ready for the next morning. Angel washed herself too and we sat around the fire in the little house the farmer had given us and we felt good. Frank had a nice shirt and an old coat that the farmer gave him and I had some clothes that the farmer's wife had given to me. And of course poor Angel had her little-boy's outfit.

The next morning came. We told the farmer where we were going and he told us, 'Stick with it, you never know, they might tell you something, there might be a way out for you. They sound like nice people and if they're any way good at all or any way fair, you can tell them what happened to you and maybe they might be able to do something for you. You never know – their people could have been in the same position as you're in today and they're back to see where their grandparents lived and where their fathers had to run from. So go for it, and go out there and enjoy yourselves. Have as much time off as you want and take them around in your pony and trap. This is a slack time of the year for me anyway; there's no hurry. Frank, you have something to do. Go and do it.'

Off we went into the town to the main square where we tied the pony. We sat on a bench and just about eleven o'clock the man and his wife arrived.

'The top of the morning to you,' called out the American.

Frank turned round and said, 'The top of the morning to you and the top of the morning to your good wife.' He tipped his cap.

She did a little curtsy. 'Oh I feel like royalty. A man hasn't tipped his cap to me in a long time.'

We laughed. The man said, 'We'll all go in the pony and trap. Would you drive around for a little while so we can see the town?'

We got into the trap and went off trotting around the town, looking at the different sights. We'd been there before so we knew our way around. But it started to rain. There was a bit of drizzle at first and then, all of a sudden, it got heavier and then sleet came. It was a very bad day, the wrong time of year for sightseeing.

The man told Frank to drive on to a hotel at the end of the street. 'There's an archway there and you can take in your pony and put him in the stables and he'll be fed and all. I'll pay.'

Frank drove us through the archway to the stables and took the pony out of the trap and pushed the trap into an opening that was under cover. He took the harness off the pony. We knew the day wasn't going to get any better so we said we'd spend a little time with them. We went into the hotel. We'd never been in a hotel before or ever seen anything like we did when we went in the door. It was something like the Big House that we'd worked in. The very same, everything in it. Heat from fires lit everywhere. It was the loveliest sight – and here I was, going in to have tea and not to scrub the floors! They brought us into the dining-room and sat us down and ordered some tea and buns.

'I think it's about time we introduced ourselves properly to one another,' the American began. 'We'll have to have first names. We don't believe in Mister or anything like that. So I'll start off. My name is Michael O'Connell and my wife's name is Mary. We have a son; he's in the army and he's coming out very shortly and his name is Michael Junior and his wife is Margaret and they've a little boy. He's called Kevin. He's our grandson and we're mad about him. He's a bit small to bring with us but please God next time we come back – if there is a next time – we'll bring him with us. My daughter-in-law had a very bad accident and she'd only the one child. She cannot have any more children. They would have liked a big family but that's the way life is. So you are like us,' he says. 'You have only one son. I've only one son and one grandson.'

Frank began then. 'I'm Frank Maguire. And my wife's name is Molly …'

All of a sudden I jumped in and said, '… And Patrick is our son.'

They looked up as much as to say, why did she interrupt? I didn't know whether I'd said the right name or what. It was looking like we might slip up. What if we had said Angel? A boy called Angel! But we settled down again. Michael went on to tell us his grandparents were buried in the local graveyard.

'I want you to find it for me. My father went on a ship all right. But he never returned because he was wanted here in Ireland and he could never come home. His mother and father and two brothers and sister died and he couldn't come home to a funeral or come to see their graves. He told me that if I ever came over here, to say a prayer at his father's grave – my grandfather and my grandmother. So here we are now and things look very strange to us. If it was now, my father could come home.'

'I think you have that bit wrong, Michael,' said Frank. 'It hasn't changed since your father left. In fact it's worse. The same people are ruling the country. You're only working here – working to oblige other people. You'll never even own yourself.'

Michael stared at Frank. 'You don't look like a man that's been harassed or had to put up with these things.'

'No, I'm not,' replied Frank, 'and neither is my wife, Molly, or my son, but I'm talking about other people not as fortunate as us.'

'But, from talk in America,' says Michael, 'I thought that the Irish are free and can do what they like and work where they like.'

'No,' says Frank firmly, 'that is not true. Those problems are still going on and will go on. I'll not see it in my day but my son might see it in his day and be free to choose and work wherever he feels like and go wherever he wants.'

'That's knocked me for six,' says Michael. 'I thought that was all over since my father's time.'

'I'm sorry to disappoint you,' says Frank. 'The big landlords are still here and that's it. You've to do what you're told if you're working for them. But we're doing our own thing.'

'Well,' says Michael, 'you're happy with that – that's good enough. Let's get back to your son. Son, why don't you take off your cap?'

Angel had got into the habit of saying 'yes' and 'no' and maybe not answering when it meant a sentence. So she just smiled and said nothing.

Mary looked round and said, 'If the boy doesn't want to take off his cap, he doesn't have to take off his cap, Michael.'

'Ah, but we usually do it in America.'

'But maybe this is the tradition here,' Mary said. 'Look, Frank still has his cap on him.'

So I tried to change the subject and asked them what it was like in America and what it was like for young people there and what way were they treated.

'Oh,' she says, 'they're educated and have everything they want, near enough. It's up to you but you try to get them everything they want. They're happy and get on with their lives doing what young people do. Getting married, settling down and having children. The same as in the other countries we've visited. But here the children seem very distant, not as friendly as we thought Ireland would be. Our people used to tell us the young people here had a great life!'

Frank butted in again. 'You're not allowed to walk on the estates or the police would be on to you. You can't go into the woodlands or you'd be accused of poaching or doing something wrong on his lordship or his lady. Only certain people are allowed do that.'

'Oh,' she says, 'I can't believe it. But I'll take your word for it.'

'If the weather takes up tomorrow I'll take you round to the big gates that are locked. Pull on the bell and it'll ring in the lodge and somebody will come out and ask you what you want. If you're well known they'll open the gate and let you in. But you can't walk round their estates or anything like that, that's out of the question. This is what I'm trying to tell you.'

✳ *Chapter 8* ✳

So the day went on and we talked about everything and anything. 'You know, it's dinner time now,' Michael announced, 'and I've ordered for you all, Frank, Molly and Patrick.'

'You shouldn't have done that, Michael,' I said. 'You and your wife have been too kind to us.'

Michael's wife laughed and said, 'I'm Mary, call me Mary.'

'All right,' says I, 'I'll call you Mary, and I'm Molly, as you know.'

We had plenty of chat. Frank was talking to Michael about America and wars. Dinner was served up and I'd not seen as much food out on a table in ages, so we ate as much as we could. Angel was very shy and I was afraid that things weren't going right, so, when she got up to go to the toilet, I excused myself from the table and I went and met her in the hallway.

'Angel, for God's sake, cheer up.'

'Mam, I'm out of place. I feel miserable and dirty. I can't stick it much longer. I hear about other young people and the lives they have in America and other countries and here I am, stuck on a farm in a strange town. I can't even go out and meet people or have any friends.' She started to cry.

I felt terrible. We had to go into a side room and I dried her eyes and said, 'Angel, don't let us down in front of those people. We want to find out about America. We want to find out what we can do.'

Well, she dried up her tears and I stood at the door of the toilet that fortunately had no one in it. This was the awkward part of pretending to be a boy.

We went back to the table and Mary asked, 'Is everything all right?'

'Yes, not a bother. We were just looking around the place. It's very nice.'

'Well, the people who own this hotel are related to Michael and they're coming over to America in a couple of years. They're going to start a business and a new life in America. They're going to sell this place and we're looking forward to them coming over with their children. They have people in America so there's no problem with them getting over there. Have you ever thought about going to America?'

'Oh, we have,' says Frank. 'We've thought about it a lot.'

'Do you have anybody in America?'

'No,' says Frank. 'I don't think that any of my people from years ago ever went over there. You see, there was only one in my family and one in Molly's family. But we would love to see America.'

Mary turned round to Angel and said, 'Patrick, would you like to go to America?'

And Angel answers, 'I would.'

'Ah, some day,' says Mary, 'you might go and do very well. There's plenty of work and a good life.'

When the dinner was over we sat back and enjoyed the chat. Frank had a smoke and Michael had a cigar. Neither me nor Mary smoked. Suddenly Michael says, 'I know this might be a bit odd, and you might think there's something strange, but would you three like to stay here with us and save the bother in the morning of having to come in? We could go off early enough if the weather's good and go out and see my grandparents' graves. There's plenty of room here and you wouldn't know yourselves! We'd all have a good rest and we'd get up early in the morning. I'll tell you –' Michael looked at Frank '– we've known you a few hours now, Frank.

We like your company and we hope you like ours and we'd just love to have a nice evening together.'

Frank turned round and said, 'I don't go out drinking because I never had the money to do so. The only time I drank was when I'd go down to the forge to the blacksmith and he'd be there with his half-crate of bottles – he liked his drink. He worked very hard and we used to have a few bottles apiece and we'd be telling each other stories and he'd be telling me how to bend the iron. I used to enjoy the couple of hours with him.' Then he said, 'If you don't mind, I'd like to talk to Molly and see what she thinks of staying on here tonight.'

'Fair enough,' says Michael. 'Talk it over, take your time.'

So Frank came over and asked me what I thought. 'We're not going to get out of this one so handy,' I laughed.

'Well,' says Frank, 'what about it? We'll stay on. It's very embarrassing to have no money but they don't seem to mind. They want to be with us and I suppose we should be glad that someone wants us.'

'Right,' I told him. 'Go back to Michael and tell him that we'll stay and have a bit of an evening with them. The farmer won't be worried and, anyway, he said to have a good chat with them and find out all about America.'

Mary came over and said, 'I am going up to my room for a few minutes but I'll be back down. I have something I want to give to Patrick. I think he'll enjoy it but, of course, he can make up his own mind about what he wants to do for the evening.' When she came back down, she had three beautiful books with her, all in brown leather. 'Do you like reading, Patrick?' she asked Angel.

'I do,' replied Angel.

'Well, there are three books here. There's one on America, one on Africa and another on animals. So you can have a good read. I suspect you want to get away from us old folk,' she said, laughing at Angel's embarrassment. 'You're probably already bored with us.'

'Oh, I'm not,' says Angel. 'But I would like to do a bit of reading. I haven't had a book in a long time.' Angel turns to me and says, 'Would you come up with me for a minute? I want you to do something for me.'

I excused myself and told Mary I'd not be long. I went up to the room and unwound Angel's bandages to release her chest. She'd been a long time sitting all day without exercising and she felt stiff and sore. I combed her hair which had grown – we'd told her 'twas dangerous to keep it long but she couldn't bear to cut it again and I didn't have the heart to force her to. It was always just tucked under her cap. There was a bathroom beside her room, so she had a wash. I stayed just in case anyone came.

She got into bed with her three books and started reading, telling me to go back down. 'Go on, Mam. And have a nice evening. I'm really tired. So I'll see you all in the morning.'

Off I went down the stairs. I felt terrible leaving her there but I knew she wanted to get at the books. We all had a great natter. I had a sherry. I hadn't had sherry in years and I could feel it going to my head, and Frank was there having the best conversation I'd heard him having in a long time. And I just said to myself, 'That's a real man, now. That's what a man should be able to do. Go out with his friends and have a chat and a drink and take the strains of the world off his back.'

As the night went on, we split up – Frank and Michael together, and me and Mary separate from them. She was asking me a lot of questions. I couldn't believe it when she said, 'Would you like to come back to America with me?'

'I'd love to,' I told her, 'but we couldn't get by all the rules and regulations. I've too many people to explain myself to.'

So Mary says, 'Well, do you know Michael is a very powerful man in America? He was a highly decorated officer in the American army and has friends everywhere. Even over here he has friends.' She paused for a moment and then said, 'You might think it's strange that our cousins, the Sweeneys, are not joining us but they're busy with the hotel till later on in the week. Then we'll have a few days with them and I hope you will come along too. Joe and Joan are the best in the world. He was left this hotel by his father to carry on the tradition but he's going to sell up and come over to America to us because he is not really a hotel manager; he's a solicitor. He's a very good solicitor and he's involved with human rights as well. Do you know what I mean?'

'I don't.' I shook my head.

'Well, sometimes he helps the persecuted and the under-dogs – put it like that. This hotel is what he has to do for now but once he gets his legal practice going well, he'll sell it and come over to us. My son will be delighted to see them. He was over here himself years ago and they're around the same age so they should have lots in common. My son Michael has a law degree too so Joe will be able to show him the ropes and he'll give a helping hand to Joe. But again, as I say, Michael Senior has great influence. He has taken a real interest in you and Frank and Patrick. I hope that we can try and get something done for you but I'll leave that to Michael. He likes to do things his own way but what he does will be perfect. He'll make no mistakes. We have been talking about you. But, as I say, we'll leave it to Michael.

'Look over at those men,' she went on. 'They're really enjoying themselves and that's the way men should be enjoying each other's company. And the same goes for women. They should have their freedom and be able to get on with life the same as the men and everyone would be happy. By the way, I think we had better go over to these boys or they'll talk all night and we won't get any sleep!'

We started to laugh and went over to the men.

'What are you two talking about?' said Mary.

'Oh, that's private,' says Michael, laughing too.

'Oh,' says Frank. 'Could you not keep away from us?'

We all laughed and had a great evening. We decided, on saying goodnight to them, that we'd all get up in the morning and do what we had to do – go out to the graveyard to see his grandparents and then take a bit of a tour around. We went up to the room and went in to see Angel. She was still sitting up in the bed reading.

'The books are great and the pictures in them are lovely. I'm really happy tonight.'

'Well,' says Frank, 'you better get asleep, Angel, because we're going out to the graveyard tomorrow. We want to do something for those people – they've done so much for us here. So we'll say goodnight!'

'I'll just stay reading for another half-hour. You go ahead.'

So we went into our room, lay back on the bed and talked.

'What are we going to do about Angel?' asked Frank. 'It's breaking my heart looking at her. She looked so pretty in her bed with her hair grown again. She's quite a young lady now. She'll be a lovely woman and will make somebody a very happy man someday. But I feel like we're destroying her life. Michael talked about America and wondered did we want to go there. He said tomorrow after we visit the graveyard we'll have another talk about America.'

'Oh, Frank,' I exclaimed, 'wouldn't that be a miracle! Could it ever happen?'

'Well you never know, Molly, stranger things happen but sure we'll just play along and do our best for them tomorrow when they go to the grave. Sure you never know.'

Very quickly both Frank and myself, not being used to having a drink, fell asleep. When we woke it was morning, but we'd had the best sleep and were ever so contented. At least we were talking to people who were no threat to us.

As we got ready that morning, a knock came at the door and there were Michael and Mary with bundles of clothes in their hands.

'We've brought too many clothes with us. Will you take some of these from us? We'll be very happy if you could. There are nice warm sweaters for both of you and some underclothes too. When you're ready, come down for breakfast and bring Patrick with you. Then we'll head off. It doesn't look a bad day at all so we can go out to see the graves. See you in the dining-room whenever you're ready.'

They went off and we closed the door and Frank started laughing.

'What is it Frank? Why are you laughing?' I said.

'Underpants!' he said. 'I never had underpants in my life! Take them out there and we'll have a look.'

Frank had tears in his eyes from laughing. He went into

the bathroom and came out with some of the new underpants on, and started walking up and down. 'What do you think of that, Molly?'

I put one of the jumpers on and later on Angel came into the room. 'Where did you get the new clothes?' she wondered. We told her. 'That's nice,' she said, 'I wish I could get some new clothes.'

'Someday, Angel, someday,' said Frank. 'New clothes and fine living. Come on down to breakfast. We've to bring those people out to the graveyard.'

We went down and it was more like a feast than a breakfast. Frank went outside and got the pony ready and brought the trap round to the front of the hotel. So we all got into the trap and away with us out to the country, out a long road. The graveyard was about four or five miles from the town and up a narrow road. Frank knew it well because he'd seen funerals going up and down to the graveyard. We went as far as we could with the trap, then had to tie the pony and walk the rest of the way.

It was very muddy and cold. There was an old man digging a grave there and Michael went over and asked, 'Do you know where the O'Connells' graves are?' And Michael told him about his family.

'Oh I do, I do. I'll bring you round and show you.' Michael and Mary followed the old man, and the first one they came to was the grave of his father's brothers and sister and just beside it was the granny's and grandfather's. Their names were carved into the big headstone. The old man went back to his grave digging and we kept about thirty or forty yards back to let the O'Connells get on with their praying. We could see the hankies coming out and it was sad to watch them. Then we started thinking about our own three boys and I put my arms around Frank and just couldn't stop crying. They spent about half an hour at the graves and then they came back to us. Michael hadn't much to say, nor had Mary. They were that sad they didn't want to talk. We walked them back to the pony and trap.

Frank brought us round by the big estate to show them the locked gates. I could see Michael's eyes glaring in at them. A very determined-looking man he was. We went to two or three of the estates that day on the side-roads. We couldn't go into them but, as Frank says, he was proving his point that Ireland wasn't free. You couldn't walk over the fields or do anything.

Michael then told Frank to head back to town. 'I've people to meet. We'll let you go back home for a day or so and we'll see what's what. We have to go to Kerry the day after tomorrow but we'll be back in a week and we'll contact you then.' Michael gave Frank an envelope, saying, 'Don't open that until you get home.'

Mary turned round and handed me another envelope. 'This is for Patrick to open when he gets home,' she said.

So we shook hands and Angel walked over to Mary and gave her a little kiss on the cheek and Mary returned the compliment. But I noticed that she kept staring at Angel.

I don't know, as I said to Frank afterwards, if Mary copped on because she was a very clever woman. She told me she used to teach children before she retired so if anyone knew anything about children it was her. Maybe we were kind of under suspicion, I thought.

We went on home anyway and told the farmer of our exploits. He enjoyed the stories. 'You've got a taste of the good life now and it's going to be very hard to keep you here. Did he make any suggestions, Frank, about bringing you to America?'

'Oh, he did,' says Frank. 'He referred to it several times in the bar in the hotel.'

'Yes,' I added, 'and I was talking to Mary and, according to her, Michael is very powerful among the Irish community in America and fairly well known here too. So they're off to Kerry and they said they'll be back in a week or so and that they'll contact us.'

'Well, there's a ray of light,' says the farmer.

The farmer's wife was delighted too. 'God is good, something might happen to help you,' she said.

'It can't happen soon enough,' I said to her. 'We just couldn't believe we could have the comforts and all that a working man should have. I know you can't do more for us but you've done a lot and we're very thankful and we'll never forget you. You're in our prayers and any other way we can help you we will.'

'It's a pleasure,' the farmer said. 'A pleasure to have you and I hope you stay here if you decide not to go. If you can go I'd love to see you make it out there. We've become very fond of you here. You're part of our family now, but Frank, keep on this man's case. When he goes back, try and correspond with him.'

We told him the people who owned the hotel were going to go to America but they didn't know when they were travelling yet and they were the only contact we'd have with the O'Connells.

'Oh,' said the farmer, 'give them this envelope and let them put my name and address on it and put a letter inside for you. That's how we'll work it. You know I correspond with America. I won't go into it but I think you have a suspicion of what we're up to with the letters going from farmer to farmer here and there. Just fend for yourselves if you can because the time is moving on. I kept the fires lit in the cottage because the weather is very bad. You needn't do anything tomorrow or Sunday. I've a few things to do around the farm on Monday that will keep you occupied but I still have very little for you to do but sure we'll talk if nothing else – you're company for me and my wife. You are good people and I hope to God that things will work out somehow for you. If anyone deserves a break, you do. You've brought luck to us and we'll do our best for you.'

'Thanks very much,' says Frank. 'We'll see you tomorrow sometime or we'll see you on Sunday and we'll tell you more about what happens to us.'

So we went on up to the cottage. Angel lit the lamp and said, 'I want to get at my books, and read for a while.'

'Someday you might read a couple of things for me.'

'Oh, I will, Mam. If you want to come up to the room with me I'll read to you.'

'No,' says I, 'you read to yourself and get the sense of the books and sure I'll get you to read to me some other day.'

Me and Frank stayed by the fire and we were sort of in a daze. But Frank suddenly said, 'Look Molly, we can't stay too long with this farmer. He's struggling as it is. I'm afraid of him being caught with us here. He'd get into trouble, even jail over it. Harbouring criminals like us on the run. They could take the farm from his wife and family. That's what I was thinking about while he was talking to me. There's something about them, the bravery of them for taking us in. If we hadn't Angel with us, we'd have no problem, no explaining to do. We have to watch what we do and say because you know what can happen. We'd be on the run again. Angel's no child now and she's feeling the pinch. We'll have to do something. When the weather picks up nearer the summer, and when I get everything done for the farmer, we'll have to head off somewhere. Somewhere we can start again.

'Frank, I'm not able to run any more,' I told him.

'Well,' says he, 'I know that. It was in your face when you were with Mary at the hotel and I was just saying to Michael to look over at the pair of you having a natter.'

'We said the same about you and Michael,' I said, smiling.

Frank started to laugh.

'You're not the only one that can talk, Frank!'

'What were you talking about?' he asked.

'That'd be telling you now. You'll never find out what we were talking about but I tell you one thing, I was very near to bringing Mary up to the room and showing her Angel. But as she was going to see her grandparents' grave in Kerry, I thought I'd have to have a talk to you first. I'll have to make my mind up. They're being very open with us, so why wouldn't we tell them about our ordeal?'

Frank said, 'I was thinking the same thing myself and coming out of the graveyard I was going to say something. They're good people and I think we're doing them wrong by not putting them in the picture, and telling them the truth.'

'We'll have to talk a lot more about it, Frank, and then we'll have to tell Angel we're planning to tell the people the truth about her. But I wondered if Mary thought that we were hiding something because of the way she looks at us sometimes. You're talking away and all of a sudden she's staring at you.'

'I got the impression from Michael that he was drifting. He wasn't listening to some things I was saying. He was looking at me, you know? He probably sees lies – he knows well we're hiding something. Something that he'd like to know.'

Angel came down out of her room. 'Mammy,' she says, 'look what Mary put in the envelope for me! A twenty-pound note! I haven't seen one before.'

'Oh,' says Frank, 'I never opened mine.'

So he opened it and there was thirty pounds in it. We were rich! We had fifty pounds between us.

Frank says to me, 'Do you know what, Molly? We'll keep this for Angel. Probably Mary expects her to have new clothes when they come back from Kerry.'

'What are you talking about?' asked Angel.

'Well, we're afraid that Mary and Michael are copping on to us and know we're hiding something from them. What do you think of them, Angel?'

'They're lovely,' she says happily, 'and they're kind and very generous.'

'And would you go to America with them?'

'I'd go to America with you two. I'd have no problem; I'd go in the morning if I could get out of these boys' clothes.'

'Go on back up to your room,' I said. 'Myself and your father are having a chat.'

'Don't sit up there all night,' says Angel.

'Now don't you either, Angel, with your books,' I laughed, and she skipped back up to her room with a little wiggle going through the door. She was some madam, she was! A really beautiful girl. She was happy with her books, and her twenty pounds. She was going to give it to me and I said, 'No, that's yours and you put that away and hide it and you'll have it one day when you want to do something or buy some clothes for yourself.'

We continued to talk through the night, and I said, 'Well, what do you think, Frank?'

'Yes,' he said, 'we'll come clean when they're back but I'll leave it to you, Molly. I wouldn't like to start telling the story again but I'll second everything you say.'

'I'll do more than tell the story, Frank. I'll show her Angel as she is. As a beautiful young girl. I don't know what way they might take it. But the people that trust us are the people we should tell.'

So we went to bed.

✳ *Chapter 9* ✳

The next morning I went down to the farmhouse and insisted on doing something to help the farmer and his wife. I washed the floors and the milk cans to give them a break. Frank went out and milked a couple of cows. The farmer was over the moon – he'd had a bit of a rest and was laughing as he said, 'It's like a hotel now! I just sit back and watch my work being done.'

He was a very good-natured person, quick to laugh and he didn't show his troubles. Sunday morning came and when we came back from the church the farmer's wife put on a dinner for us. I could have cooked it myself so I insisted on going in and giving her a hand with it. Angel went out and fed the chickens and did the little jobs she used to do every day. She loved the animals – the pigs, sheep and lambs. She was very close to nature. But she was getting to be a big girl and growing up quicker than we expected. That Sunday night me and Frank called the farmer in and told him what we were going to do.

He sighed a bit and then said, 'This is a hard job you have. I can't advise you or disagree with you in any way. I think your decision is right. I don't know how the Americans will take it. You could be digging a hole for yourselves and getting into trouble. Or else, this could be your freedom you're looking at. So the decision is yours but I'll stand behind you whatever decision you make. I can give you a reference for what it's worth – that you're good people but, with the problem of your daughter, the main thing is that if you could go to America you'd be free. You'd never have to look back, but you'd look back in anger at what was done to you and what's still happening to people here in Ireland. It'll never go out of your mind. Anyway, me and my wife will support you any way we can.'

Then Frank told him that they had given Angel twenty pounds and himself thirty.

'My God!' said the farmer in amazement. 'That's a fortune. I wouldn't even get that in a year on this farm. They must think the world of you all. Well, we do too.'

'I'll second that,' said his wife. 'You're lovely people and you need a break and deserve a chance. This could be it, or it could be your downfall. We can't advise you, as my husband says, but we can pray that things turn out all right for you. There's bound to be a light at the end of the tunnel. But as far as telling the people about your plight, they might just back you up. And if they do, you'll be right. They seem to have power and good connections. You can't turn down this chance. Have your story right. Don't hide anything – just tell the woman. She'll listen and she'll remember every word you say.'

We said goodnight to them and went back up to the cottage. Angel was there combing her long blonde hair. I looked at her and said, 'We want to talk to you, Angel. This is very serious and please don't interrupt till we're finished. It all depends on you.'

'What's so serious?' she said, looking worried. 'Were we caught? Is someone coming for us? What's wrong?'

'No! Not yet ...' I said quickly, '... not yet.'

And Frank added, 'All you have to do is listen to your mother. She's going to ask you something and see what you think of it.'

I told her what I was planning to do with Mary and Michael when they came back, that we thought that it was only fair that we were straight with them.

'I want to show them how beautiful you are and that you're a girl ... and a lovely girl. I have to trust someone.'

'Oh, Mam,' she said, her eyes shining, 'I'd love that. I can't pretend much longer. They're very kind, lovely people and I don't mind them seeing me as a girl or hearing our story. So yes! I'll go to the hotel with you when they come back and I'll show them who I am and see what they think.'

I told Angel what the farmer had said about digging a hole for ourselves, or that the Americans could walk out on us and never see us again, or maybe tell somebody about us, but that we had to take that chance because they were the friendliest and most trust-worthy people we'd met outside of the farmer and his wife.

'I don't know,' says Angel, looking serious, 'I think they'd be shocked all right but they'll get over it. At least you'll know where you stand. Now I know how to spend my fortune! I'll have to get a dress – but where are we going to get it? We can't go round the town to shop. Someone might recognise and report us.'

'Angel,' said Frank, 'we'll go to another town and your mother can dress up. She got some nice clothes from Mary. I'll drive you there; it's about ten miles from here and you can get all you need, and you can dress up in the house. I'll get the farmer to change this money into smaller money because they'd wonder where we got the big notes. We must dress up the best we can so they think we're small farmers or something. I'll still have to get more money …'

'Oh, I'll pay for them,' interrupted Angel.

'No, you won't. You're keeping that. I'll give you the money for the clothes. I want you looking the best, and up or down, we'll go together.'

'I'm happy with that, Dad,' she laughed.

And I said, 'Right, we'll do it. I'll ask the farmer tomorrow morning if we can go off. I don't think there's very much to do anyway.'

The next morning Frank went out to the farmer and told him what we were going to do. He asked if he could have the twenty pounds changed to small money for the shop.

The farmer was delighted. 'I've change in the house. We've a handbag here belonging to my wife that you can bring so Molly can look the part. There's nothing wrong with you – it's not the way you look, it's the way you feel. And if you feel everyone is watching you, try to stop thinking like that. Off you go to the town!'

Frank came back to the cottage and told us what the farmer had said and handed the handbag to me. 'Now you're a lady, you've a handbag!' he laughed.

Angel started laughing too. 'Mam with a handbag! What are you going to put into it?'

'Oh,' I says smartly enough, 'I'm going to put plenty into it.'

We had loads of laughs as I strolled up and down the floor with the handbag. Then Angel had a fit of giggling, pointing her finger at Frank.

'What's so funny?' he wanted to know.

'Oh nothing, Dad'

'Ah now,' says he, 'come on and tell me, what's the joke?'

'Mam said you got new knickers off Michael!'

'Don't mind your mother!'

'Oh, I heard you were marching up and down the hotel room showing them off, how fine a man you were.'

'We'd a great laugh that night,' I said. 'Very happy we were because we knew they were going to do something for us, something important. It's a long time since I shopped and so we're going to make a good go of it.'

We were very cheerful as we went off the next day. It took us a few hours to get there and we went into the square – the usual place where people shop. Frank went off walking round having a look in the windows. Angel and I went into a ladies clothes shop and did a bit of shopping; got a nice dress for Angel and some underclothes and all that women need. The shop assistants kept looking sideways at Angel because she was very poorly dressed since she had no girls clothes. The dress I got from the farmer's wife was years old, from when she was a thin young girl herself, and it was kind of swinging loose on Angel. But we got by. They just thought we were country people with no dress sense. Like Mary had said to me in the hotel one time: some people have no dress sense. I hardly understood then what she meant, but I do now!

So I got everything we wanted. Frank had a parcel with

him too. He had bought himself trousers and a new cap and an overcoat. I had bought a few things for myself as well. Then we got back into the trap and headed home. We arrived home late that evening and we pulled up to the cottage and me and Angel went straight in. Frank had to feed the pony and put away the harness. The next thing the farmer's wife came running into the cottage.

'What did you get? Show me, show me!'

Sure Angel was delighted and so was I to see the farmer's wife take a great interest. She made Angel put on the dress.

'Oh!' she says, clapping her two hands together. 'She's beautiful! Isn't she, Molly? She is absolutely beautiful. That's a lovely dress and lovely clothes that you got her. She's going to impress those people when they come back. No matter how bad you think things are going to go, I tell you, when they see her, they're going to forgive you for not telling them. And please God they might see what I can see in her. She's a beautiful girl and she needs a chance. She needs friends and to get out and about – she can't hide for ever. So when they come back, you're going to see that they will take to her. Maybe they know already, maybe they have some suspicions. Or maybe they think that this Patrick is a bit queer in the head or something. We were talking all night about it, afraid something would go wrong. I'm glad you're back with the clothes. And sure Angel's delighted! She has everything a young girl needs now and I hope all goes well for you.'

'It will,' I told her. 'You're very good to us too and we won't forget it.'

'Oh, I know that,' says the farmer's wife. 'All I'm saying is I hope you have good luck. Just in case, when you see Frank tonight – he's down in the fields but he'll be up shortly – if anyone comes here to the farm and wants to know your names, Frank is to be Sean Joyce, you're Bridget Joyce and your son is Patrick Joyce. You were born in Connemara in the west of Ireland and you travel around from town to town, do a bit of work and travel on. Tell that to Frank. We have to have the story right. Are you clear on that now, Molly?'

'I am, yes. I'll tell Frank when I go up.'

Off she went and soon afterwards Frank came in the door. He brought his saws and hatchets to sharpen and get ready for chopping wood and cutting timber for the farmer.

The next morning we went off about our work. Frank went down to the fields and Angel fed the chickens and calves, throwing in a bit of hay here and there. I was in the house doing the washing, helping the farmer's wife. She wasn't too well at times but she still worked hard and I used help her when I could.

Suddenly Angel, who'd been down at the farm gate which led to the laneway that brought you onto the main road, came running in screaming, 'The police! He's coming up the laneway on a bike! He's coming for me! What am I going to do?'

'Calm down,' says the farmer's wife. 'Don't get excited. You go into the room with your Mam and stay quiet and don't open your mouth.'

The farmer came running in the door with Frank because they had heard Angel's screams.

'What's up?'

'The policeman is coming up the avenue. Have your story ready, names and all. Go out and be doing something in the yard and Angel and Molly hide down in the room. I'll talk to him.'

So the policeman came up, greeting the farmer with a 'Good morning!'

The farmer answered him back very friendly. 'Good morning, Constable. Is there something up?'

'Eh,' he says, 'his lordship's timber was taken last night and there was four lambs missing and poaching going on in the rivers. I hear you have a Traveller working for you and I want to see your pile. If there's no fresh timber in it, I can eliminate you off me books.'

'Go down the yard there to the shed to the left-hand side. It's all my own timber off my own land. I don't take timber from anyone.'

'I'm not accusing you.' The policeman nodded. 'But even so, I have to check it out.' So he went off down the yard, had a look around and came back.

'Could I have a word with you? What's your name?' he asked Frank.

'Sean Joyce,' Frank replied quietly.

'And what's your wife's name?'

'Bridget Joyce.'

'And your son?'

'Patrick Joyce.'

'Where do you come from?'

'The west. Born in Connemara, on the roadside. We go around from place to place all over the country, doing a bit of work and travelling on.'

'Well,' says the policeman, 'I don't like you round here at all and neither does his lordship in the Big House. He doesn't like to see you round here because you're only trouble.'

'I'm just helping out the farmer,' said Frank. 'He doesn't give me money; he just gives me food and a roof over our heads for the winter and we do the work.'

'Well,' the policeman goes on, looking hard at Frank, 'I don't like them getting too friendly with the likes of you. You should be run out of each town you go into.'

'I'm sorry you feel that way,' answered Frank, tersely.

'That's the way everyone feels, especially his lordship. They've no comfort with you, every time he sees you in the town or sees you hanging around.'

'I'm sorry about that,' says Frank. 'We'll be moving on as soon as the farmer is finished.'

'The sooner the better,' says the policeman. 'Because I get

sick when I look at you, annoying his lordship and big people like him and being around his land.'

'I work for my living,' says Frank.

'I've heard enough now,' snapped the policeman back. 'Don't give me any of your backchat. When you're finished here, you go off and bring your wife and child with you. We don't want you round here.'

He went back down to the farmer who asked, 'Well? You talked to the hired help there.'

'I did and I gave him his marching orders.'

'I need him here,' the farmer told him. 'My family is away at school and I need him and my wife needs that woman in there to do work that she isn't able to do. Near the spring or into the summer he'll be going off about his business. I'll get a fresh one in then.'

'You're very fond of the Travelling people, aren't you?' remarked the policeman.

'I am not! But it's a way of life for them. What can I do? I need him. You know what I mean, Constable. I keep them busy. Isn't that the right thing? He'd be too tired at night to go anywhere and so is she and the young fella. They aren't able to go anywhere because they worked hard all day till dark at night. And that's the way to handle them. This fellow seems to be sticking it longer than any of the rest of them. But sure he'll get fed up and run off some morning.'

'Ach, indeed he will,' admitted the Constable, 'and the sooner the better.'

'All right,' the farmer says, 'good luck and goodbye now and mind yourself on your travels.' The farmer's eyes were not very friendly now. As if to say, well is that what you think of us all? Once the policeman was gone out of sight, Frank came and told him what was said and the farmer told Frank about his own talk with the policeman.

'I told him I worked the hands off you and you'd be too tired to go anywhere, and he agreed with me. That's the way to deal with them, he said. That's all they understand and that's the way to do it but don't keep them too long. And I told him I was getting a fresh one in as soon as you go.'

So Frank and the farmer started laughing together. It was kind of a little victory for the farmer. But it was too near for comfort and Angel couldn't sleep that night. She was afraid. Every bump she heard in the night she'd wake up and sit up in bed frightened. She knew it had been a close thing.

'Is it going to happen one of these days? Will we ever see Mary and Michael again? We mightn't get the time to explain to them.'

'Well,' says I, 'in three days they'll be back and all will be revealed. That fella won't be back again.'

'Are you sure that he won't be back, Mam?'

'Not till after the spring. In the summer he'll be wondering why we're hanging on so we have a decision to make.

We're not going to upset you anymore – just leave it with us and we'll do our best Angel. You're not to be afraid.'

'Well, I'm afraid something will happen to you and they'll put me away or they'll put me back onto the estate again. I don't want that. I don't know what I'd do if you were taken from me and I was put away.'

'I'm afraid too,' I said.

Even Frank agreed. 'We're all afraid, so you're not alone. But we're going to do something about it and stop worrying, because we're worried when you're worried. So just read your books and don't pass any remarks on anything. I'll do the talking. No matter who comes in, don't you talk. Don't open your mouth to them. You can just brush them off. We love you and that's all that matters and if we go down, we'll go down together.'

❈ *Chapter 10* ❈

*T*he next day we worked as usual. We had two days to go before we would see Michael and Mary again and things were getting a bit tense. We were tired and hadn't slept very much. We were thinking of the Americans coming back all the time and what might be said and how they were going to take it. We'd put ourselves into our situation and we had to get ourselves out of it one way or another. Without Michael and Mary we'd have no clothes, nothing really, and they'd given us a great time.

We were even more tense the following day – the day before Mary and Michael were coming back. We didn't know what day we were going to hear from them. They just said they'd contact us when they got back and they'd tell us how they'd got on. We were looking forward to seeing them and breaking the news to them. We would put it straight to them to find out what they could do to help get us to America, if anything; all our chances were in those two people. No one but ourselves knew that they were our last hope. The last chance of survival. The day was very long – every day was – because we were that anxious, waiting, wondering would they come back, wondering would they come near us at all? We were afraid behind it all that maybe we'd blow our chance and blow Angel's chance for a decent life as well. That was our main worry.

But Angel was confident that they'd come and see her again. She was waiting for them. She liked them and she had her twenty pound as well so she was over the moon waiting. She knew what we were going to do: show her dressed as a girl, show that she could enjoy things that other young people could enjoy. I found it sad watching her waiting.

Two days went by and we knew they should have been back. I was washing clothes inside when somebody knocked at the door. It was a young boy on a bike.

'Is the farmer around?' he asked. 'It's a letter for him. Will you give it to him?'

'I will,' says I, 'I'll give him the letter. He's down in the fields and the missus is not here.'

'All right,' says this young boy. He was a grand young chap and pleasant. 'Make sure he gets that letter.'

Frank and the farmer came back after a couple of hours. It was near dinner time and I had the dinner ready for the farmer, Frank, me and Angel, but the missus was in town. She'd a sister there and she used to go in and see her every week or so.

'There was a boy here and he left a letter for you,' I said.

'Oh did he?' says the farmer, taking the letter from me. 'What was he like?'

'A young slim boy and well dressed.'

'Ah sure, let me look at the letter anyway.'

So he opened the letter. 'Well,' says he, 'it's not for me, it's for you and Frank, and says would ye come out on Saturday afternoon to the hotel where they're staying. You'd be staying a night or two or for whatever time they've left I suppose. So that's good news for you.'

We looked at each other, me and Frank and Angel.

'Oh my God, we're definitely going to face it this time.'

'That's no harm,' says Frank. 'We'll face the music and that's all about it. So don't be losing sleep over it and you too, Angel. It's us that's responsible for what we're doing, not you. You're the victim in the whole lot and you've played the boy well and it's time to come out in the open. We'll all be happier once we tell these people the truth. I don't think we can be selfish. We have to concentrate on Angel and that's all there is about it. We'll try it and we'll see what Michael can do. Is he as powerful as Mary told you, I wonder? Now, I believe them and I hope they will believe us. They might have heard such stories before, you know. They'd get kind of wise to it and think we're looking for something or trying to get a handy fare over to America or something. Maybe they'll just tell us to go home, that they don't want anything more to do with us. What have we to lose, anyway? That they might tell the authorities and get us caught? That's not going to happen – they'd be more loyal than that. They are honest people and they look like people that hadn't it easy either. But we're going to take a chance on it, Molly, for Angel's sake. They like Angel a lot. We just have to wait and see … I'm tired, Molly.'

'So am I, Frank,' I said to him after that long speech.

'I'm going to my room,' Angel said. 'I'm going to read another book tonight.'

'And have a good rest,' I said, 'for when we go in on Saturday you'll want to look alive because all will be revealed then and hopefully they won't hold it against us for telling them the lies. They can judge us if they want to.'

On the Saturday morning we got ready. Frank shaved and I washed myself. We got our clothes and things ready to bring into the hotel. We didn't know whether we'd be staying there or not once we'd broken the news to them. Angel was very excited. She had great faith in what was going to happen that day. She dressed up as the boy, but I put all her clothes in a little bag. So at half-eleven that morning, we set off in the pony and trap for town.

When we arrived, Frank didn't take the pony out of the trap because he wanted to see what would happen first.

'Frank,' I said, 'I'll handle this. You don't say a word to Michael or anything. I'll handle it with Mary. Woman to woman. There'll be three women – Angel, Mary and me – so we'll be the majority. We'll rule!'

We both laughed. We went into the hotel to the reception area and the man at the desk told us that Mary and Michael would be down in about five or ten minutes. There was tea ready for us in the lounge.

The Sweeneys came over with the buns. Joe and Joan were very nice. They went off about their business and we waited for Michael and Mary to appear. They came down the stairs all of a rush shortly after, and came straight over, clearly delighted to see us. All that went on in my mind was, would they be as nice in another short while when we've told them everything?

They poured our tea and began telling us about the graves they visited and how sad they were. But they had met nice people down in Kerry and Mary had met some friends. Some of them had been in America before and many were going back.

Mary was in a rush of talk and excitement about the trip: '… and it was great to see them again. We really enjoyed ourselves, apart from seeing the graves. Just like Michael and his people – he was a bit upset that day and it takes a little while to get over it, you know.'

After a couple of days sightseeing with them and looking in the shops and places like tourists ourselves, and after loads of tea and talk one day, I turned to Mary and said: 'I'd love to have a private talk with you, Mary.'

And Michael laughed. 'Is there privacy going on now? I'd like to have a word with Frank too. You and Mary go off and sure Patrick can stay here if he wants.'

'No, I want to bring him upstairs with me. He wants to see the piano.' I had to say something like that to bring Angel upstairs. I didn't want her around Frank and Michael.

So Frank and Michael went off down into the lounge and me and Mary and Angel went up the stairs. They had a room down at the very end of the corridor and we had a room facing Angel's room.

'I'm going up to my room for two minutes to change this jumper. It's very warm,' Mary said, and she went off down the corridor. I went into Angel's room.

'Now,' I whispered urgently to Angel, 'dress up, comb your hair and look your best. When I call you into the room I'll be telling Mary the truth. We have to do it now.'

'Good,' says Angel. 'New shoes and all! I'll be ready in twenty minutes. You can call me in and we'll see how Mary feels about the way we misled her.'

'You go on now,' I told her. I went into our own room and

put my hands over my face. I couldn't hold back the tears and the more I tried to the more they came. I was shattered. Next thing, a knock came on the door and there stood Mary in a dress. She looked well in it – she was a lovely looking woman.

'Molly, what's wrong?' she cried.

'Come in.' I motioned her into the room. 'I have to tell you something. It's been playing on our minds since we met and especially since you went off to Kerry. We're going to come straight with you and tell you our story – the whole truth. You have heard some of it, but you're going to hear everything this time. I hope you won't feel bad about it or resent us in any way over it. We only did what we did to protect someone we love very much.'

'It can't be *that* bad,' Mary said, looking a bit puzzled. 'We did a lot of things together, and had lots of conversations. Sure we nearly know everything about each other.'

'No, Mary,' I told her, 'you don't know everything. We know your story as much as you told us but you don't know ours. We had to hide our story from the whole world, not from you alone but from nearly everyone.'

'I don't understand,' says Mary. 'You seem so happy, you and Frank and Patrick.'

So we talked a bit more and she made me dry my eyes. She sat on the bed and I sat on the chair beside it.

'Are you ready to speak, Molly? Are you ready to tell me

all about this terrible thing? Or did we do something to you?'

'No, no!' I exclaimed. 'Mary, we think the world of you and Michael. And of the Sweeneys. They were very nice to us too. You're the first people we've ever felt comfortable with since we've been on our travels.'

'On your travels?' queried Mary.

'Yes, travels. I've a little surprise for you. And you can explain it all to Michael tonight, or sooner if you feel like telling us to go away. Everything depends on you and Michael and what I'm going to tell you and what I'm going to show you.'

'Well,' says she, a bit impatiently. I knew she was taken aback at what I was saying. 'Come on. Spill the beans. What have you to say?'

'Sit there on the bed for a minute, Mary. I want to show you something.' I went out to the corridor and rapped on Angel's door.

'Are you ready?'

'I am, Mam,' she answered. 'Did you tell Mary?'

'Not yet. I'm going to show you to her and see what she thinks. We may get turned out of the hotel over this but we have to be fair to them.'

I walked to my room and Angel followed behind me. 'You come in in a couple of seconds,' I told her

I opened the door wide and went to the chair and sat

down. Mary kept watching the door. And in walks this tall girl, with long blonde hair and a lovely dress and socks and shoes on her. She stood in the doorway.

'Oh my!' cried Mary. 'What a beautiful girl! Is this your child?'

'It is,' I told her, trying to smile as I said it. 'Her name is Angel.'

'Well, she's terribly like Patrick!'

'I'm going to tell you something, Mary. That is Patrick. But really it's Angel. She's my daughter. We've been hiding her for the last few years and pretending she's a boy. And we told you she was a boy. You were very nice to us and ...'

Mary just fell back on the bed and she cried bitterly, and I said to Angel, 'We must have given this woman an awful shock.' She just wouldn't stop crying. She cried and cried and cried and the black stuff she had on her eyes was running down her face. She got up and put her arms out to Angel.

'Come here, sweetheart. Come here to me.' And she held Angel and hugged her and hugged her and kissed her. 'This is a terrible thing that was done to you. I hope there's a good explanation for it. No one would ever do that to my child or my grandchild. There is a grave injustice here. Oh, but you are beautiful. You were beautiful as a boy too, but the day we were going away when you kissed me on the cheek I felt a tenderness ... I could feel the femininity between us but I didn't pass any remark. I thought it was just me. I'm shocked to see you standing here now, as a girl. It's something that we mothers dream of, to have a lovely girl with long hair and beautiful features. No mother would do what was done to you unless the reasons are very, very strong. Bind you up and keep you as a boy? Molly, before you explain all this would you go down to the lounge and bring me up a half-bottle of brandy and a bottle of sherry for yourself and bring some lemonade up for Angel – as you call her now. Because I need a drink! I feel weak at the knees; I don't feel well at all.'

'Fair enough,' I agreed. 'We've been living with it for years but we will explain. At this minute Frank is explaining everything to Michael. I can tell you the story as well and if the two stories are different, you won't want to see us again. We haven't rehearsed anything. It's just that we had to tell you what was happening in our lives. I hope that as a teacher and as an educated woman you will listen to us. We have proof of it. The farmer we live with and other farmers on the way from here to Meath.'

'Where's that?' asked Mary.

'It's up beyond a place called Dublin.'

'Oh, Dublin.'

'Well it's on beyond that about thirty miles. And that's where we started. Well, we came from the Midlands and went to Meath, then ended up coming from Meath down here to Cork. But I will tell you the whole story and see what you think. And it'll be entirely up to you and Michael whether we're friends and whether you want to be our friends again or not. I'll go down to the lounge now and I'll be back up as soon as I can.'

'Don't draw the attention of the boys,' Mary called to me at the door. 'Leave them where they are and in their own time they'll come up or call us down. Just keep out of sight and bring up the drinks.'

I went down into the lounge and stood at the side of the bar where a young girl was serving along with Joe Sweeney. The young girl was coming over but Joe said, 'No, leave that to me. I'll serve Molly.'

The bar was packed. There was an awful sight of people in it and families. Down in the far corner I could see Frank and Michael very deep in conversation. Well, Frank was; Michael had his hands under his chin, holding his head up, staring at Frank as he was talking away.

Joe came over to me, smiling.

'Are you enjoying yourselves?' he asked

'Oh, we are.' I smiled back.

'I'm sorry I can't join you. Myself and the wife are very busy here and we're a bit short of staff. We'll have a night with you and Michael and Mary before they go back. You know I'm going over there?'

'I heard that, Joe,' I told him, 'and I wish you the very best of luck.'

'Oh God,' he said with a knowing smile when I asked him

for the drinks, 'Mary must be really on it tonight. She doesn't usually drink brandy but if she wants a half-bottle, she gets it and you'll want a sherry and the young fella – I'll give you a large bottle of lemonade for him.' So he put half a bottle of brandy on a tray and the lemonade and the bottle of sherry. 'Anyway, enjoy yourselves. Do you want me to tell the boys you're here?'

'No, no …' I said. 'Don't say I was down at all. It's just, Mary wants to talk.'

'Oh indeed, abandon the men! Plenty of gossip.'

'Yes, plenty of gossip is right.'

'If you like I'll bring that tray upstairs for you; it's a bit heavy.'

'I'm well used to carrying trays up and down stairs, so it's no bother to me,' I told him.

He laughed and I went on about my business up the stairs and into the room and put the tray down on the table.

Mary asked me to fill her out a drink so I poured some brandy but she said, 'Come on, a bit stronger now. Again!' So I filled it three-quarter way up the glass and she waited till I filled out mine and Angel filled out hers. We felt great at this stage. We'd got some of our tale out, anyway. Mary took a big slug of brandy and she drew her breath and held the glass – I thought it was going to break in her hands. She looked over at me and said, 'I forgot to say good luck – that's what we usually say.'

So we tipped glasses. We didn't know what you were supposed to do, never being drinking people before.

'Are you ready?' Mary said.

'Are you ready to hear the story, Mary?' I answered her.

'Well I am, but wait there for a minute while I go to my room. I'll be back and then you can continue.'

Mary went off out down the corridor into her room and was back a few minutes later. She brought this little case. It was full of little paints and powders and lipsticks and I had never seen anything like it.

'Do you know what I'm going to do now? I'm going to make up Angel to bring out the colour in her eyes and her skin, while you're telling me what you have to say. I want Michael to see her at her best.'

I didn't know what she meant. She got her chair out and Angel sat down.

'Oh,' says Angel excitedly, 'I read about this in a book one time. About people putting make-up on their eyes and …'

'That's exactly right!' Mary said to her. The first thing that Mary did was to start combing Angel's hair and then brushing it. She had brushes of all descriptions with her.

I started the story. I kept talking. I started from the beginning. I was there talking away and at times I thought she wasn't listening and then she'd say, 'Go on, I'm listening.' She'd even interrupt me the odd time and say, 'Go back on that, say that again.' And I'd say it again and then she'd say,

'Go on from there again.' But she kept listening. I thought she wasn't at times but she was listening to every word. I kept talking and talking and she kept combing and got these little brushes out and she put powder on Angel's eyes. I'd never seen her looking as beautiful in all my life. But these creams she put on Angel's face made her look like a film star.

'Now,' says Mary, 'isn't that more like it, Angel?'

She brought over the glass for Angel to look in it.

'I wouldn't know myself,' whispered Angel in awe as she saw herself in the mirror.

'Oh you do, that is you. You're always going to look like this.'

'I don't know about that,' says Angel, 'not while I'm hiding in this country.'

'No, but in the next country you go to and, if we have our way, that'll be America. Your mother and father and yourself. You'll be able to mix with young people of your own age and go cycling and swimming and horse riding and all the things young people enjoy. Everything you want to do, you can do. I have a vision that things will look a lot better to you this time next year. This is what I want for you, Angel, and for your people, having listened to your mother telling her story. Here, I just want to give you something else.' She took a nice necklace out of a box. 'I wore this as a young girl going to college and I'd like you to have it. Just turn round there and I'll put it on.' So she put it on Angel. It was gold, with a little cross on it. 'I want you to have this because I always meant, if I had a daughter, to give it to her. You're the nearest thing that I have now to a daughter so you can have it. And there's other things but they'll wait till I'm going. They'll be your little personal belongings. Something to remember me by. No matter what happens, I'll make sure that you're looked after. This should never have happened to you.'

She took a red ribbon out of the box and tied Angel's hair loosely with it and pulled the hair down around her face. This woman was well used to parties and dressing up. Angel thanked her and sat down looking in a mirror. I kept talking the whole time. I was trying to get everything out in the open. It was coming up to three o'clock in the morning and there was no sign of Frank or Michael still. I came to the end of my story and wasn't able to go on any more. My eyes were tired. It had been a long night and it was very hard telling Mary what we'd been through.

But she helped me out. 'Go down to the bar and see if those two fellas are drunk or what are they doing and bring them up here before Michael gets too drunk to see Angel like this. You can tell me the rest in the morning. We'll be up at about eleven o'clock. I'll never forget a word of what you've told me.'

So I went down the stairs and there was no one left in the lounge but Michael and Frank. They were still talking.

'Are you not finished talking?' I asked. Michael looked

up. His eyes were red, probably from the drink I thought to myself. Frank looked exhausted. Telling our story to people who had never heard it before was not easy.

'Mary wants Michael up in the room. She wants to show him something. And he's to come up now.'

'All right,' says Michael, 'I'll go up.'

'Well,' says I to Michael, 'I know what Frank has been telling you and I've been telling Mary.'

'I can't believe it! It's an outrage!'

'Don't talk about it any more, Michael, just come up with me now and you come up as well, Frank.'

We went up the stairs. We went to our room and let Michael walk in front of us to see Mary smiling there, standing with her arm across Angel's shoulder.

✳ *Chapter 11* ✳

'*G*ood luck to you, my dear!' Frank said to me when we were back in our room alone later on. We had drinks in our hands and we were tipping our glasses happily.

'Good luck to you, sweetheart,' says I back to him. 'And by the way, Frank, where did you learn all that nice talk?'

'Below in the lounge. That's the way they were treating one another and sure I'm romantic too, you know!'

We laughed and drank our drinks. We put our arms around each other and after a while we did something we hadn't done in years – we cuddled up together and had a lovely night. All our worries went away for that night. Next morning Frank says with a smile, 'Well my dear?'

'Well, sweetheart!' I answered. 'And did you enjoy the night?'

'Lovely. We must come here a lot oftener than we do.' So we laughed again and I felt so happy. It was all because things were out in the open and a big strain had been lifted off us.

Our story was told. That was the first time we'd had real contact with each other for a long, long time, and it felt lovely. But we didn't discuss it any further. We had to get ready for the road, have our breakfast, go back out to the farm and tell the farmer all that had happened.

Mary was already in Angel's room and was sharing her breakfast tray with her. Mary had fallen for her and so had Michael. They were treating her like their own. We were delighted because we knew that whatever chance Angel had was with these people or people who they knew. The kindness was in them so we were happy enough.

'Good morning Frank, good morning Molly,' called Mary. 'I'm looking after Angel here.'

'Oh yes, we can see that,' we said together.

Angel laughed. 'This is lovely, Mam. I could get used to this kind of a life.'

'Maybe you could,' Mary said to her. 'But we have to discuss something before you make a move this morning. We're off down for our breakfast but we'll have a talk when we come back up.'

So me and Frank and Mary went down to the dining-room. Michael joined us too – he had been in the bar talking with the Sweeneys. Joe and Joan came over and had a cup of coffee with us.

'Now, Molly, about Angel …' Joe began. He told us that he'd take care of her at the hotel, that she could stay there till something could be worked out for her. 'Would you agree to that? I don't think it's a good idea for her to go back to the farm and I don't think she'd like dressing up as a boy again, anyway.'

'I'll get rid of all these clothes,' Mary piped up, 'because it's not fair.'

I looked at Frank who said, 'I don't know. We'll have to talk between ourselves over this, and talk to Angel. It's a very serious move – if the policeman came back to the farm, he'd probably look for the boy. We'll talk it over if you give us the time.'

'All the time in the world.' Michael stood up. 'There's no hurry on you out of here today but, when you're going, Mary and I will go back to the farm with you. We want to talk to the farmer.'

'I hope you're not going to say anything bad about us,' laughed Frank.

'Indeed I'm not saying anything bad about you. Joe will bring us so you can go ahead in the pony and trap. We'll come out later on. Tell the farmer we're coming to have a chat with him. It's just something personal we want to talk to him about, nothing bad about you or anything. He knows our families and we know his and he has family in America too, but the farmer's hands are tied there as well. As you say, Frank, the law is coming back to see that you move on.'

'I know that,' says Frank, and I told him that I knew it too. 'But we will have to discuss what you have in mind with Angel. So how will Angel get by here?'

'The first thing she'll be taught is how to be a waitress – not a slave or a skivvy or washing floors. She's very intelligent. She'd learn how to serve tables and how to prepare tables and it'll be good training for her. Mary will help her out with her books and explain how the world works. She seems to open up to us and maybe what she needs is someone to prepare her for the life that's ahead. She's been through the mill along with you but she knows things will be different. Of course, you will have to talk to her and tell her what you want her to do, and what we're going to do for her. But we will still be working on your case as well to see if we can do something for the two of you.'

We finished breakfast and Joe said, 'I'll see you in a couple of hours' time. I have a few things to do and I'll meet you down here and you can tell me what you decide to do about Angel. I'll go along with whatever you want to do, but myself, I can't see her dressing up as a boy again. So it's entirely up to you to convince her and maybe you'll have no convincing

to do with her. I'd like Mary to have a talk with her after you
have finished because she likes Mary and she likes Michael
and she sees the goodness in them and I think she likes us
too. We'll do our best for her.'

So we talked to Angel to see could we persuade her to stay
on and help out in the hotel whilst things were developing.
She has a long life in front of her, we told each other. 'A lot
longer than we have,' I said. We went upstairs to her room.
Angel was reading her book and eating a bit of toast. She
was like a lady in the bed. And we were joking with her,
calling her 'Madam' and asking, 'Have you enough to eat?'
We always had a good laugh with her.

'We have something to discuss that is important. We only
have the one shot at this. We don't want to be doing anything
wrong because we feel we done enough wrong already.'

'You did not, Mammy,' she says. 'You and Dad are the best
in the world to me. You only did things for my own good. I
know that.'

'I'm going to ask you something now and if you agree, I
think you could take a load off all our shoulders and your
own. This is about your life and your future so think carefully
before you answer.'

'I will, Mam,' she agreed.

'What do you think of you staying here? Or do you want
to be dressed up as a boy again and go out on the street with
us this morning and go back up to the farm and carry on

the way we were? Or would you like to stay here and learn to be a waitress and how to cook and do all the hotel work? To stay here as a girl? Or come back to the farm with us as a boy? Now, we're not deserting you or anything. We'd always come in to see you but we have to be very careful that no one realises what we are doing. Down there in the lounge, they think that you're Michael and Mary's grandchild and Joe and Joan's cousin from America. Truthfully, Angel, what do you want to do?'

She looked at us, her eyes open wide in surprise. 'I don't want to go back to the farm as a boy. I want to stay as I am now. I would love to stay here and work in the hotel and learn the trade, do cooking and table-serving and setting out tables for big parties and things like that. I'd be very happy here so long as you come and see me. I don't think I can carry on any longer as a boy. I feel happy here, and I should be working anyway. It doesn't matter about the money. It would be good for me to get some sort of trade.'

'Well, that's grand!' I said.

Frank began, 'So you'll stay here. But you'll have to be very careful who you're talking to, you'll have to get to know people's names and who they are, but not ask any questions. Joe will show you the ropes and Joan'll tell you who's who that comes in and who you can talk to and who not to talk to. Just in case there's a slip-up, because that policeman is going to come back and he is going to look for the boy and his mother because he didn't see him that last day. I didn't like the look on his face and I'd say myself he will be back because he wants us to shift on. We'll make a story up that you went off with Traveller friends of ours and that you'll be back in a few months or we'll catch up with you because you got fed up hanging around.'

'That's great, Dad,' she says. 'You have your story right anyway.'

'That's settled then, so long as you're happy,' Frank said. 'But if you feel unhappy, you'll tell us won't you?'

'I will Dad, I'll tell you. Don't worry about that. I'm going to miss you but sure I'm used to this big room already, and I'm used to the bed. I'm not far from you so you'll be able to come and see me any time you like. I can meet you anywhere and we can even meet outside the town where we went for the clothes.'

'I don't know about that,' Frank replied. 'They're still looking for a man, a woman and a blonde girl and they can judge what age you should be and what you look like now. They'll want to know where the boy is gone and how we come to have a girl. The posters are still up. You've seen them too Angel, and you know what it says on them. That's still hanging over our heads. They have no intention of giving up looking for us because the last day I went by the police station I saw a fresh poster up and I know just to look at it that it's us they're talking about. They think we're telling stories about how they treat the people in the Big Houses and what they do, so everyone is keeping a lookout for us – all the big shots around. The people here are sound and good and they're trying to free people like us so we can live our lives with our families. You'll have to be very careful. We couldn't come into this hotel when Mary and Michael go back because they'd wonder where we get the money to be in a hotel. If they see us with you, they'd put two and two together again and catch us. But Angel, that's our problem. We will get to see you and if you get lonely or anything, remember we'll be with you because we'll be thinking of you every hour of the day and every night. Your bed will be empty, but we'll be thinking of you in the cottage. There are people who are trying their best for us and one day we could be free. We might get to America. We mightn't get off together, but we will end up together.'

'I know that, Dad. Mary was telling me all about America and about people she taught. She was at their weddings and confirmations and first communions. She was happy to see them doing well in life. If I ever go to America, I could be one of her pupils. She would help me get through to high school and to college.'

Frank laughed. 'College?'

'Yes, Dad. College! I'd love to go. I'd love to be with the rest of them going off to school and high school and then college, and then being somebody like Joe. Being a solicitor or a teacher.'

'By God,' exclaimed Frank loudly, 'you have high hopes for yourself.'

We had a good laugh; things were sorting themselves out.

We had to give those people an answer and it had to be a final answer so I said to Frank and Angel, 'We can't go back on our word, and Angel, you can't go back on yours. We'll have to be very careful going back to the farm from here or they might notice you're not with us. We will have to keep out of the town till they forget about us. We can keep our heads down. We will come to see you but not together. Your father this day and me the following day, something like that. I can see the policeman coming back looking for the boy and his mother just to see their faces, to see could he make something out of it because Travellers are well noted in police stations and post offices. Even in the grocery shop you would be copped on, going in and out – they would get to know you. You know the score yourself. So that's your answer? You'll stay on here in the hotel?'

'Yes, Mam, and thanks for everything you're doing. I know I'll be lonely but I know that we'll all be safe this way. And you're only a few miles away. I think myself that Joe has the right idea and Mary and Michael like us. Especially Mary – she tells me stories and helps me read and everything. She has great time for me. In fact, I wouldn't mind going to America with them.'

So I asked her, 'You'd go to America on us?'

'Well, you'd come with me, you know.'

'That's good enough. We'll go down and tell them that you decided to stay here.'

'And tell them I am very thankful for the offer and I'll accept it.'

We got up to go and she said, 'I had a great dream last night.'

'What did you dream of, Angel?'

'I dreamed of the boys,' she said, 'and they were laughing and happy and everything and I was telling them about the time I had and they were laughing and they were dancing round me and everything and all of a sudden I woke up! It was only a dream but I think myself that they are happy.'

As we went down to the lounge, Frank says, 'I had a feeling that she was going to mention the boys.'

'I know that, Frank,' I says. 'I was going to mention it myself to her but I am glad that she sees them in a different light now. That they are happy and contented in Heaven. I believe God sent her a little message that he is looking after her brothers.'

'Molly, I think we should stop talking about the boys and carry on with what we are doing here now. We might be upset enough with leaving Angel after us without having to carry the three boys with us too. We'll go down and break the news to Joe and everyone.'

We went into the lounge. They were sitting down having coffee and we went over and they sat us down.

'Well?' asked Michael. 'What's the answer?'

Frank sat up. 'Michael,' he says, 'she'll stay here and do whatever Joe wants her to do.'

Joe put his arm around me and Mary turned and put her arms around Frank, and Michael butted in on all of us and didn't we all shed a few tears. Joe's wife Joan came over and joined the party.

'This calls for a very special drink,' said Joe. 'It's something to celebrate!'

He went in behind the bar and took out a bottle. They called it champagne and the cork struck the ceiling. He filled little glasses out for us and we toasted one another. 'Here's to a long life and a good future,' said Joe. We all joined him in that and we sat down again and Joe went off with Joan up to Angel's room to welcome her into the family. We stayed there with Mary and Michael, sipping our drinks.

'That's a start,' Michael smiled at the two of us. 'You have a bit of lunch and make your way back to the farm because the evenings are short. Just tell the farmer that we will be out later on. I'll go out in the car with Joe and Mary to have a chat with them. Joe knows them as I told you, and his wife knows the missus.'

We had lunch and went up to see Angel before we left. She looked very happy. No tears, just joy in her face.

Joan had dressed her up in a waitress' outfit. She looked lovely; you would want to see her! She was the loveliest waitress you ever seen, and she over the moon with her little uniform.

'We start from here,' Joe told her. 'We won't have you working anywhere else, just on the tables, and my wife will show you how to set tables and we'll tell you who to speak to and who not to.'

'I know,' says Angel, 'my Dad and Mam told me all that. I know what you mean.'

'That's great,' says Joe, and he and Joan went off happy.

Michael then told Frank, 'I think you should be on your way now and I'll see you later on this evening at the farmer's house.'

'All right,' says Frank. He shook hands with Michael and kissed Mary and I kissed Michael and Mary and Angel. We weren't saying goodbye. We just said we would see her later on and she was happy enough. She walked down the stairs with us and she turned at the bottom of the stairs into the dining-room where there were other girls working. We looked in after her and there she was, talking away as if she had already forgotten about us. We were very happy for her. She was amongst girls like herself who wanted to get on in life and were willing to work hard to get by.

We went out and Frank put the pony in the trap. I got in and we went off back to the farm. I went into the farmhouse and Frank went off up the yard with the pony to take the harness off him and put him into the stable.

The farmer's wife asked me, 'How did you get on? You must have had a great time. You look very well.'

They were laughing together with me, the farmer and his wife. Frank came in and the farmer shook hands with him and the wife gave Frank a big kiss and says, 'I think you must have struck gold!'

'We did, we did,' we both said, laughing at ourselves. So we told them what had happened and that Michael and his wife and Joe at the hotel were coming out to see them.

'That's great,' he says. 'Joe and I know each other well and I knew Michael's people. We'd better take out the best delft.'

He looked at his wife and they were smiling. They were delighted to be getting a visit from these very important people. We went on up into our cottage. The farmer had the fire lit. He had kept it lit the whole week and the place was lovely and warm. We looked into Angel's room and we burst out crying. She wasn't there, just her old clothes.

'Now,' says Frank to me, 'we better stop this crying game. We better get everything about Patrick out and burned. There is an old barrel out there for burning stuff like that and we will burn every stitch belonging to her when she was a boy – the boots, everything.'

So we gathered up everything she had, the little things that were in her room. It was heartbreaking but we burned all Patrick's stuff. That was the end of Patrick as far as we were concerned. We had our Angel back again. But there was nothing here belonging to her, nothing to say there was anyone in the room. That was heartbreaking. Still, we had to do it. We had done the same with our boys' clothes when they died. At least this time the person who owned the clothes was still alive and going to make it in life. We sat there for a while and Frank smoked his fag and I said, 'You know what, Frank, you'd miss the sherry and the brandy, wouldn't you?'

Frank started laughing. 'Now don't be tempting me. You know me when you get the brandy in me!' We laughed all night. We couldn't look at one another with the laughing. We felt like two teenagers in love again. We could hug and kiss. It felt good to hug each other although we were missing Angel. But in truth we had missed each other's company as well.

Even when we had a family, we still were in love and the bad people of this world tried to take that little thing from us and they nearly succeeded. But thanks to the farmer and his wife, and Michael and Mary, and Joe and Joan, we got some sort of a life back and some of our love back. Though in truth, that was something that no one could give you. It had to come back itself. But we got a good start with those people.

We were sitting there thinking about going to bed when

I said to Frank, 'They're very late coming out. Michael and Mary and Joe, you know.'

'Eh,' he answers, 'look out the door and see if the car is there. Sure with us acting the eejit here, they might have come in unknown to us.'

I looked out the door and I could see the car at the farmhouse door. 'Frank, they're down there. We never heard them.' That'll tell you how much fun we were having and how relaxed we were. Before that we'd hear every crack in the timber, we'd hear every bit of tin that moved or anything that stirred in the yard. It just shows what a little bit of kindness can do for people.

We waited up another while anyway and put more wood on the fire. We were relaxing at the fire with our arms round each other when a knock came to the door. Michael and Mary were standing there along with the farmer and his wife and Joe and Joan. So they all came in and sat anywhere they could find a seat to sit on.

'You're very comfortable here,' says Michael.

'Thanks to the farmer there and his wife we have this bit of comfort,' I replied.

'Well,' says he, 'we have been talking and the farmer and his wife here are very happy with you and give you the highest recommendation. And they're glad to see Angel as a girl again.'

'She will do well,' says Joe.

'Of course she'll do well,' Joan added. 'Isn't she one of us now, one of our own? She'll come out top of the class yet. Even as we were leaving this evening, she was polishing the silver and wouldn't stop.'

'She is well used to hard work,' Frank agreed. 'The farmer and his wife would tell you that. She'd feed the pigs and the calves and she'd sweep the yard and she'd do a bit of housework.'

'That's right,' said the farmer's wife. 'She's the best in the world. I'd be proud to have her but circumstances don't allow that.'

'We are thankful to you too,' says Frank. 'You have been great at understanding.'

'But,' says the farmer, 'you are an honest man and you are not a coward, Frank. You are not afraid of hard work and you helped me out a lot here and I won't forget you for it. You are great working people. You appreciate what people do for you. Although you say little, you know a lot. You're a man that can keep his mouth shut. I watched the way you handled that policeman. You could travel Ireland and still get by and no one would know you. You never let anyone get inside that skin of yours!'

And he laughed. 'People are going to change this country. As Michael here says, it's a blight we have here in Ireland, the abuse people get. Michael maintains it is an illness in these big people. You lost your family and your livelihood for nothing. You are guilty of nothing and no one will ever convince me or anyone else that you are guilty of anything. You are guilty of being honest and guilty of being poor.'

Joe turned round and spoke up. 'The people that cause these injustices can't hide their activities much longer. The truth will come out in the open. I don't know how long it is going to take, but their secrets will come out and the shame of it will destroy them. They wrecked your family and weren't too far from destroying Angel too. I hope everything works out well, Frank. I dread what I'm thinking now – that things might backfire on us. But I suppose everything will be all right, Frank, so long as Angel is taken care of. There's more people like Michael and Mary out there; that's a great thing to know.'

'That's right,' says Frank. 'I was thinking the same. We are lucky we met you all. I was often sorry when things were bad on the road, but now I can see a ray of hope and a bit of a future for us all.'

✳ *Chapter 12* ✳

A bit of wind blew up and flapped the canvas noisily. Molly stopped talking for a while. She sighed a couple of times and Frank turned to her.

'Molly,' he said quietly, 'I think we have told the boy enough for now. It's getting late and it's getting very cold. The fire is going down. I think Pat would want to go home to his people now and have a think over what we told him.'

'Do you think you've enough of it, Pat?' Molly asked me. 'I wouldn't blame you. The story's not over yet but we don't want to bore you with our problems further if you don't want to go on with it.'

'Molly,' I told her, 'I could do with time to think back on what *you told me. It's a lot to take in. But I want to hear the rest no matter how long it's going to take. I want to take it all in and not forget any of it. So I'll say goodnight to you and Frank and I'll see you the day after tomorrow for more of the story.' I stood up to head home.*

'Goodnight,' said Frank, 'and thanks very much for the coats and thanks very much for listening. You're a good lad to come down to hear our tale. As Molly says, it's not over but there isn't that much more left.'

I said goodnight to them both again and I went off home.

I was off work the next day and went for a walk over the fields. I sat down on a stone, thinking about what the Travelling people had told me. It was really getting to me and I couldn't sleep with their story going over and over in my mind through the night. Apparently, the most interesting bit was still to come. Perhaps the saddest part too, I suspected. I wanted to hear the whole story, to remember every detail so that I wouldn't make any mistakes in retelling it myself. The people that I'd be telling it to might need convincing.

Although I was very young then, I'd heard lots of stories. But I'd never heard anything like this one (nor have I since and I hope I never will again). I knew too that there were other people who suffered the same sort of treatment in those big estates, but who weren't around to tell the story, or who couldn't or wouldn't tell out of fear. So I decided it was up to me to do it for them.

I went back the following night to hear the rest of their account.

Maybe, I was thinking, I could help the old couple somehow or other. I didn't work in the shop at night anyway, so down I went.

It was the worst night ever. There was sleet, snow, rain and wind. It was terrible. My raincoat hood was up but the cold came right through it. I reached the tent and I tapped on the top of it.

'Is that Pat?' Molly called out.

'It is, Molly, it's me.'

'Isn't that an awful night?' she said, opening back the flap to let me inside. 'Do you want to catch your death of cold?'

'I had to come down anyway, so here I am,' I told her.

They had no fire lit because with all the rain around it wouldn't light. I moved up to the end of the tent and Molly shifted some of the clothes to make room for me. I thought to myself, what a different world altogether; could this be real? How in the name of God can these people survive in weather like this?

'What do you think, Pat? What do you think of our home?' Molly asked me.

I didn't want to embarrass them, so I said, 'Oh, it's grand.'

'I never got used to it,' she told me, a kind of sadness in her look.

'Neither did I,' added Frank. 'But we have our privacy here and there's no one to bully us or tell us what to do. We're kind of in our own world here. The only way we survive is this little tent and our fire and a few utensils for cooking. But you needn't think that you'd get used to it Pat,' he went on, 'because you wouldn't survive here after the comforts of your own home and your nice bed and your bedclothes.'

I said nothing for a while. Then I just said, 'Please God, something will happen and you'll get a place and you won't be afraid or have to run any more. Times are changing.'

'The times won't change fast enough for us,' Frank replied, 'but it might for others. It might for others. People should be able to live happily and not be in fear.'

We talked for a while but it was stuffy in the tent. I was trying to imagine what it would be like with children and babies like most Travelling families would have. The rain could keep on for days or maybe weeks and you could hardly ever get outside, and you'd be wet and cold, and hungry because you couldn't cook a meal. You could do nothing until the weather let up. I had never even thought about it before.

We finished early that night and without continuing the story for they weren't in form for talking, what with the awful cold and damp. They were wrapped up in the old coats I had given them, and they had a few bits of blankets. I even felt a bit damp where I was sitting.

When I got home, my mother had a big fire on and I sat staring into it. She asked me if I was OK. 'Pat, you don't look very well.'

'Ah,' I shrugged, 'I think I'm coming down with a bit of a cold. I'll be all right tomorrow.'

'Go off to bed and I'll bring you up a hot drink,' she told me.

So I said goodnight to her and my Dad and went up to the room but I couldn't sleep. I couldn't stop seeing Molly and Frank lying in that wet ditch with only a few coats over them and the rain lashing on the canvas. I could hear it then on the windows of my room. It left me more determined than ever to go back down the next night. There was justice to be done for them but what or how I didn't know. I just knew I had to hear the whole story.

Morning came and the rain, snow and sleet had stopped. After dinner that evening, off I went again to Molly and Frank. They had the fire lit this time. It wasn't a bad night; dry but very frosty and cold.

'I was thinking of both of you last night,' I told them.

'We were thinking of you too, Pat,' Molly said, 'about how good you were to come down to us in the spills of rain and snow and sleet. We won't be around for much longer but it keeps us going, telling you what we've had to go through.'

And we settled down so she could continue.

Me and Frank were going about our daily work at the farm. We often met up in the yard and had a chat. We were doing a lot more talking than before and were getting very close again. The farmer loved to see us wrapped around one another. Even though we missed Angel terrible every day, we were happy for her and no longer so worried as knew she was well looked after.

I was walking back to the farmhouse one day and I saw a

young boy coming up the lane on a bike. When he came to the gate I opened it.

'Is the farmer in?' he asked.

'He is, son. Just go ahead on up to the house.'

He went on up on his bike. I had seen him before when he'd been out here with messages for the farmer or his wife. Anyway, I watched him hand a letter to the farmer and then he got on his bike and went off again. I told Frank the boy was here again, and that he gave a letter to the farmer.

'Molly, don't be saying anything. Just pass no remarks,' he said quickly to me.

Anyway, after about ten minutes, the farmer's wife came out and called the two of us in. She had a big mug of tea apiece for us and a few sandwiches. At eleven o'clock in the morning we always got that. The farmer took out the letter. It was from Michael and Mary.

'They are coming out tonight and they are bringing you off to a hotel, lucky you! I'd love a night or two out myself.' He was laughing away. 'You'd better get your glad rags together tonight for you're not coming back till some time tomorrow.'

'I wonder what they want,' says Frank.

Anyway, the day went by and we got ready. We could see the lights of the car coming up the road that night. You had to be very careful it was people you knew before you'd appear out. They blew the horn and I went down and opened the gate. It was Michael and Mary driving their cousin's car. We shook hands and kissed as usual and were delighted to see each other. Michael explained that they had been very busy but had seen Angel every day and that she was getting along brilliantly at the hotel. We got into the car and headed off. We travelled for miles and came to a town and parked the car at a small hotel. We went into the lounge and of course Michael had everything organised as usual.

'Come on down to the restaurant. I've ordered a meal for you. I want you to meet someone.'

We went down and there she was – with a lovely suit on her, real ladylike, with a red ribbon in her blonde hair. She looked like someone I had never seen before, did Angel. She was stunning and, by the look of her, she had grown another couple of inches since we had seen her last.

It was weeks since we had seen her. There were things happening, and things being arranged for America that we weren't told much about, but we had been told not to go into the town. She hugged us and kissed us and was a bit tearful but sure so were we. It was an awful shock to see our little child so grown-up all of a sudden and she so beautiful and everything – it was hard to take in. We asked her how she was getting on and she began explaining to us about the silver and how they cleaned it. After half an hour or so we joined Michael and Mary and sat down to a big meal.

Angel said, 'There is someone else here I want you to meet.' Another young girl came over and Angel introduced her as her best friend in the hotel. 'Me and her walk together,' Angel said. 'Her name is Ann and she's from miles away from here too. Joe and Joan are looking after her as well. I'm very happy here but I think of you every night and every day and wonder how you're getting on.'

'We're getting on great, Angel,' we told her, 'and we're glad that you're settling in.'

'Well,' Angel said, 'it is grand now until Joe and his wife and children move over to America. Then I am going to be alone again. I don't know what to do. Joan says we just have to wait until the time comes.'

She was talking like a girl of twenty-five or twenty-six – too serious for her age. But we knew that with the hard times she couldn't be any other way but grown-up. She asked about the farmer and his wife and about the chickens and pigs and calves, and about the horse and the pony. So we filled her in on everything.

We had a happy evening. We were told that we had to stay in the hotel that night. Angel was being collected by a friend of the Sweeneys so that we wouldn't be seen together. Mary said she would bring Angel around the town to the shops. 'She is my friend now and I'm very proud of her and pleased to be able to do this for her.'

'I know that, Mary, and we're very proud that you're with

her. And Michael too,' I assured her. 'I hope you'll always be friends.'

'We will,' says Mary, 'and if it is left to us she will be more than a friend and so will you. But we are saying nothing now. Michael wants to have a few words with Frank to explain what is happening. So we will go off and have a sip of sherry. Angel is with her friend so we can have a bit of a natter. I think the boys will be talking business. We'll go and have a drink before we go to bed, Molly.'

We stayed in the lounge and Frank and Michael moved to a corner where they could talk in private. I sipped port and Mary sipped brandy, and Angel was talking to her new friend. I had never known her to talk as much as she did with this young girl. They would get up and wander around and come back. They were two right madams to look at! Beautiful. Frank and Michael were over in the corner, drinking and talking very seriously. I couldn't wait. I wished the night would move on so I'd hear about what was being said.

Mary suggested we go to our bedrooms and finish talking in the morning. I went into Angel's room to see that she was all right. She was very happy, but a loneliness was still in her eyes – I could see it. There was a mix of sadness and happiness there. I stayed about a half an hour with her and then I went over to my own room and waited up for Frank. It was nearly two in the morning when he arrived up from the lounge. I could hear Michael bidding him goodnight.

Frank came in and I asked him how he got on.

'Very well,' he said. 'We had a great chat and things are going nicely. You know, Michael doesn't give you too much information, well, not information that I could understand. But he is doing something to help us. That is what he wanted to tell me – not to despair. Just wait and carry on as we are. He's waiting on word from America, from another relation of his that worked in immigration. And he's waiting on word from the fella that worked in the registry office in the town that we were in, and he's caught between the two of them. But he's not going back to America till he's got something sorted for us.'

'I'm retired anyway so time doesn't matter,' Michael had said to Frank. 'I miss my son and my grandson and my daughter-in-law. But even so, I think they understand. My son knows what's happening. He knows that I always help people out if I can and especially our own so I am going to wait here until I get everything fixed up if I can, and if I can't it won't be my fault. I'll give it my best shot. It's not doing a good turn, it's a Cause and I must see this through. Mary is willing to hang on as long as it takes until we manage something for you and for Angel. We just couldn't go back to America without seeing you right. You're our friends now and I hope you feel the same.'

'We do,' Frank had said to him. 'There is nobody like you.'

'Well, there we are then. I'll see you in the morning. I might hear something tonight. I've to go back down. I've to see the manager of this hotel. Everywhere I go, I am expecting to hear something from someone. They won't talk to you Frank, but they will talk to me. They know who I am and they know what I am and I don't like taking no for an answer.'

'Are you sure there is nothing else?' I asked Frank, and he told me no, that Michael was going to take each day as it came.

'You know, Molly,' he said calmly, 'we could be in America in a few months' time with Angel. Free as the wind.'

'Frank, I think we shouldn't count on that yet,' I told him. 'It doesn't look like that from where I am sitting, even though I have plenty of faith in Michael and Mary and in the Sweeneys. We'll just keep our fingers crossed and keep on working. Angel is safe. She's beginning to be noticed in the town now with Mary and Michael, so she is safe. And even if they go back, they'll think that she is staying on for a prolonged holiday. She's safe whilst we don't hang round her because it would just look too out of place for us to have a beautiful girl like that with us, and we working for nothing, only our food with the farmer. We will be moving off shortly is what they think but no matter where we go we will have to leave Angel after us. I don't think that she would want to come anyway, to go through what she went through before.'

'I know that,' Frank agreed. 'I have no intention of disturbing her. Michael was telling me that she is learning everything very fast. She is quick on the uptake and she needs school and college. He said she'll be a brilliant student, but for now they're just doing their best. That is what he says anyway.'

'That's something,' I told Frank, 'because there is no one else going to help us.'

'Well, Molly,' he smiled, 'I'm going to go to sleep. I'm tired and I'm not used to this drink.'

'That's OK,' I nodded. 'We'll have our breakfast and sneak off the way we sneaked into this place, without Angel. Things are working out for her.'

The next morning Michael was up before us and before Mary. He was in and out, in and out, talking to this fella and that fella in the lounge, and getting on well with everyone. He came over and joined us for breakfast.

'You know,' he says to Frank, 'I did well last night when I went down, and I did a little better this morning. But I am not saying anything to you yet. It's early stages but things are looking bright. After breakfast I'll take you back to the farm. We are going to send Angel home with a friend of the Sweeneys, herself and the other girl. They have to get back to work. As I told you Frank, I am not giving up. I haven't even started rightly on your case yet, but your story has gone out to the relevant people so I am waiting on word. I'm even more anxious than you are but you mightn't think it. Say goodbye to Angel too for it will be a week or so before you'll see her. We might have to change our venue. You don't know who comes in and out of these lounges.'

And I thanked Mary for looking after Angel.

'I teach her reading and writing, and a bit about America,' Mary said proudly. 'She's a star pupil and I hope I live to see the day she graduates. I'll be the proudest woman in the world and Michael the proudest man.'

All of a sudden the door opened and this tall man came in. A bit of a gentleman type, very well dressed and a hat on him and a coat. He walked up the lounge and said, 'I'm looking for a Mr Michael O'Connell, an American.'

'Here,' said Michael, and he went over to him. They were talking for a couple of seconds and the next thing the hands went out and they were shaking hands and clapping each other on the back. They stayed talking there for about five or six minutes before Michael came back and said to Angel, 'My lady, your car awaits. This man is taking you back to Sweeney's hotel and your parents are going home.'

Angel kissed us goodbye. We told her we would see her in a week or so and we were happy for her. Her friend came over and kissed us goodbye also. They went off then with the gentleman.

I asked Michael, 'Who's that gentleman?'

'He's important to me and my family. He's looking out for

you as well as for Angel – you don't have to know any more. The less you know, the less you can explain to anybody. But he is well known to us and we to him. It is not everyone we trust Molly, and with your story we trust even fewer. So the best thing you can do is forget what you've seen, heard or done. Off in the car now with us and we'll take you home to the farm and I'll see you in a few days. If I don't come out, Joe will. We will always be in close contact. This is a very busy time, so don't think when you don't see me coming that there is nothing being done.'

They took us home to the gate of the farm. The farmer's wife came running out, eager to hear any news. 'Come on, tell us how you got on. You had a great time – I know by the look of you!'

She brought us into the house and made tea. We told them all that had happened but we didn't mention the man collecting Angel and her friend. The farmer asked about Angel.

'She's great and looks lovely and is more like a young woman every day. Looks like she grew a couple of inches and she's filled out. We are very happy for her,' I told him.

'You don't have to worry anymore,' he said. 'I know everyone in that hotel. And I know the man who left Angel and her friend home. He is a good friend of mine too.' He started to laugh. 'Aren't we a peculiar sort of people, us Irish? We love keeping secrets from each other.'

Frank started laughing too. 'I have very few secrets after last night because I don't even remember going to bed.'

'You're getting too used to the beer, Frank. That's what's up with you. You're getting to like it.'

'I'm barely able to drink it and I was never a man for the heavy sessions,' Frank admitted.

'You'll get used to them,' nodded the farmer wisely. 'If you ever get to America you'll get used to it. Yourself and Molly will have a great time.'

We had a good laugh. Then we went back up to our little cottage.

'There is no use starting to talk about it,' I said to Frank. 'We'll get into our working clothes and help this man out. Just as Michael says, we'll have to take each day at a time and leave it to them. We're doing no good talking about it. We are only raising our hopes.' So we carried on with our work that day, and night-time came as usual. We heard nothing for about four or five days.

☀ *Chapter 13* ☀

*W*e had more visits from Joe Sweeney, always with a good word about progress. When a car would pull up at the gate we'd always think it was Joe, but sometimes it wasn't. Lots of people came and went on bikes or walking but we'd mind our own business. It wasn't right to go spying on the people who were our saviours so we'd wait and see if the caller had anything to do with us. Then we'd be brought down to the parlour where all the talking was done, with a drop of whiskey or a cup of tea. One time Joe had a whole lot of information about checking registers and birth certificates, who was christened and where and by what priest, and they wanted dates and all sorts of information. Paperwork, he called it. They seemed to be well organised. Frank and me were happy to let them at it for we couldn't do anything ourselves except answer questions as best we could. 'Twas clear though that this wasn't the first time they had done all this kind of stuff.

Then one evening we were collected by a driver in a lovely big car with leather seats, and we were driven about thirty miles, down a long avenue and up to the door of a very big farmhouse. It was dark by then so all we could see was the shadows of cows and sheep in the fields.

'Call me Philip, and I'm supposed to keep my mouth shut,' the driver said to us in a good-humoured way, 'but you're coming to my house so I know all about your suffering and we're all on your case down here now.' Michael, Mary, the Sweeneys and some people we didn't know would all be there.

At the house a girl took us to a bedroom as we were to stay the night.

The next day we had a long chat with Philip and what he told us amazes us still. 'You and your Angel are safe here with us. We all admire what you have done, and your story is the people's story. It is the story of a Cause. The Cause is what we give our time and money to: the cause of the downtrodden people of Ireland. What you two did – the fact that you walked out, and why you did – was brave and risky; but still you did it. That is a great tale for ordinary people, and we want to make sure you get the freedom you have a right to. You are not any landlord's chattel, and we want to be able to tell your story all over the country. There are plenty of people still in bondage to these big estates and landowners. You survived where many wouldn't, with nothing in your pockets. You slipped their nets and the police, and here you are, still ahead. People love a fighter and you fought and you've won out so far. We'll see you get further. Your example will motivate others to resist.'

We didn't know what to say back to him. We went in with him to the front room, where we saw the O'Connells and the Sweeneys and a few people we didn't know. Philip told us we were still waiting for more people to come.

Mary came over to me and took me to one side while Frank and the other men went off to another room to talk. 'It looks like you're doing plenty of talking and he looks very confident in himself. Like a leader he is, just like the rest of those men there. He seems to have come out of himself.'

'Well, I'll tell you one thing Mary,' I said to her, surprising myself with what I was saying, and I don't mind repeating it either, 'he's my hero and he's Angel's hero. He's something that every woman wants in a man. He's true and he's loyal and he's brave. Yes, I can be thankful for what I have. No matter what happens, I still have an angel. That makes life worth living because there are a lot of other people who are not with loved ones tonight.' I was talking and talking.

'You took on something, Molly; you took on people who were wronging you. You both did it and you can be very proud of Frank,' Mary said.

'I am,' I assured her. 'Just the same way as you're proud of Michael.'

'I suppose they've something in common,' she answered, 'but we'll say no more for now. We'll have our tea. We're still waiting on this man to come. At least we'll see who it is anyway and maybe we'll be a lot wiser when he goes away again. They're all very anxious about whoever's coming.'

Mary took my arm and we went over to the table to have tea. We were talking to the other women, exchanging little stories about family and friends. I felt very comfortable with them. They seemed to be just like myself. And there were no whispers nor anything behind our backs. They were very open and the lady of the house was the best in the world. She had done her utmost to keep us happy. She knew me and Frank were waiting; we were more anxious than anyone to hear what was going to happen. But we had to wait.

By half past eight everyone was getting tired. Where we were eating, you could see out the window so Mary kept looking out every chance she got. I wondered what was on her mind. Eventually, she said there were two cars coming up the driveway. We all felt excited and stood up to look out.

'You'd better step back from the window and pull the blinds,' said the woman of the house. That was because people coming and going didn't like to have people watching them. 'I'm used to it myself,' she told us, 'and I'm used to minding my own business. That's the way we have to carry on here.'

We all sat back at the table. Some drank tea, some coffee and some had a drink. I wasn't in the form for a drink because there was too much on my mind. The cars pulled up at the entrance and we heard the doors open. Six men got out – we could still see them at the side of the window – and they went into the room where the other men were.

After another hour, we were all called down to the men in the main hall where the big dining-room was. There the six men stood. They were well dressed and had these little cases with them. Frank and Joe Sweeney and Michael and another man we didn't know called me and Mary over. The six men who had come in shook hands with us and one of them stepped forward and said, 'I want to meet Molly.'

So I stepped forward and said, 'That's me.'

'I'd like to have a private chat with you and Frank and, if everyone excuses us, we'll go into the front room. I just want to introduce myself and tell you why I'm here and who I am and what I am.' He turned to the others. 'So excuse us for a few minutes and then we'll get on with our business.'

We went into the front room with him. He put his hand out and said, 'Sit down, I want to explain who I am. The ship I came in on was delayed – I should've been here yesterday. My name is Father Tom Miller. I was born and reared in

America and I'm a good friend of Michael, Mary and the family. I came over on a fact-finding mission from my parish in America to find out what's happening here and what we can do for the people. And especially what I can do for you and your daughter. I believe you have a lovely daughter called Angel. Michael and Mary have put me in the picture. Michael's son and his wife told me to tell you they wish you the very best of luck. Any time you come over to America, you'll be welcome and they will look after you. These five men outside who came here with me come from five different parishes in Ireland. They are going to take me round the different places. They will take me to each of their parishes here. Some of the men cover two or three parishes and there is one particular man who has seven parishes to cover. The bigger the parish, the more work they have. We know you cannot trust everyone, but I am a priest and I am going to listen to you and I am going to try and help you the best I can.'

He stopped and looked straight at us for a moment. Then he went on. 'Now to business. I know you come from Meath but which parish do you come from? Who was the parish priest? Who helps out in the church and does the general work and what are their names and where can they be contacted if I need them? I want to hear about your own story, and why you are not registered anywhere. I believe from Michael and Mary that the world thinks you are dead and buried a long time now, but in my eyes you're no ghosts but people who've been through the mill. I will do my best to help you out. Now I cannot work miracles, and sometimes I have to hide my priesthood to help people. I know that God might never forgive me but then again, he might.'

He started to laugh. 'You know people here are very afraid of the clergy. I know that. But not all priests are bad, nor all Protestant ministers either. The priests and the politicians and the police hold a key to whether you succeed or fail. I'm here to discover for myself. But nobody knows I am here – I'm incognito. Only a couple of people from my parish and a few people here in Ireland know who I am. That is why I am not dressed as a priest. I'm thirty-four now and I have been a priest for a long time. Michael and Mary will tell you – I am their parish priest, the man who looked after them and their family all these years. So I want you to trust me as you trusted Mary and Michael and the Sweeneys. If you give me that trust, it will help me to understand what happened to you. I need to know what I am doing. I can't afford to slip-up. If I do I could be in awful trouble for helping you. But worse, the people I deal with would definitely be in trouble.

'My grandparents came from Ireland and I feel as Irish as any of you. Now, I will get on with my work as soon as you tell me the names of the parish, the parish priest, the people who help him with his paperwork or who clean the church, for instance. I would be very interested to know if Angel is registered in that church. Did someone write her birth in the register and if not – you might think this is strange – it might be all the better. I must be one hundred per cent certain her name is not in the vestry book there in any shape or form.

'I know you trust no one from that area – Michael and Mary told me in their letters – but is there anyone at all you can trust or is there anyone you know that might take the chance and do a bit of work for me? I can't wear my clerical dress so they will have to trust me too. If I am found out, it mightn't be very pleasant for me either. I put my name down as Tom Molloy and my story is that I am over on holidays from America, and that I work as an engineer on the railroads. This is who I am to you now and to anyone who asks you.'

We sat in silence for about five minutes. I would look at Frank and he would look back at me and we would shake our heads. Tom Molloy, the priest, kept staring at us. He was a lovely young man, very focused, and his eyes were very determined. He left us alone for a few minutes, then came back in again.

Frank turned round and began, 'Well, Father …'

'Now, before you say any more,' interrupted the priest, 'I'm Tom and don't forget what I'm telling you. I'm Tom. You don't know me outside this house tonight. Don't be calling me Father. Just call me Tom. Get used to it and remember that name – Tom.'

'All right,' says Frank. 'I don't like calling you Tom because I have great respect for your collar but if that is the way you want it, OK. I had only one friend up there and he might help. I'm nearly sure he would help. He was the only man that I trusted with my story. He made the cross for my dead children.'

'Who is he?'

'The village blacksmith, Ned Donoghue. I don't know whether he is dead or alive now but he used to shoe the parish priest's horse for nothing and his wife used to help in the vestry. And she would wash and iron the clothes for the priest. I don't like asking those people to do anything because they are in as much danger as we were. But you came a long way to do a very risky job. I might be a lot braver than you think Tom, but I wouldn't go back over that road again or I wouldn't go within forty mile of the village or the farm or the church where we brought our children to Mass.'

As Frank spoke, the priest was writing down notes.

'I understand,' said Tom. 'I understand what you are saying.'

'But it doesn't mean that we fell out with God. We taught Angel the best we could about religion. She was the only one that questioned why God was doing this to us if God is so good.'

'Oh,' said Tom, 'everyone feels that way at times. I often thought He'd forgotten about me. I don't think we will ever know the answer.' Then he went on: 'This is going to take a bit of time. I've only two months and I can't give all my time to one case. As I go into the different parishes and the different churches, I make sketches so I look like a real tourist. I will make my way to this blacksmith and I will ask him if he will help us. So I say goodnight to you now because in the morning I will be on my travels. I'll be in Meath soon. I'm on the road early in the morning. It is a pleasure to meet you. You are brave people and good people. You still held on to your religion in difficult circumstances. I can trust you to say nothing. Goodnight and God bless you until we meet again.'

He left the room and closed the door after him. Frank and me sat there and we looked at one another.

'What do you think, Molly?' Frank says to me.

'I don't know what to think, Frank. That is the first time ever a priest sat down and talked to us instead of trying to run us down or make us do things that we didn't want to do. I could have told him anything.'

'The same with me,' says Frank. 'We never had a priest who sympathised with us, only criticised us for not doing things by the rules. Having lost our boys and all we had, we were supposed to start another family immediately. Like an animal in a field. I think this man will go as far as he can to find out whether Angel is in that book or whether they know about her at all. As Tom said, all the better if she's not.'

'How do you make out that, Frank?' I asked him.

'They might give her a name with some family. Now I am only saying that, Molly. I would hate if she lost our name – and we'd be forgotten about and couldn't call her our little Angel again. Maguire mightn't be a lucky name after all, but even so it is the name I was brought up with. I am proud of it. My people and yours too, Molly. They got by struggling but they got by. They died young from hard work and hardship. They were just scraping the bottom of the barrel each day. I want to sleep on it, Molly. Things always look better in the morning.'

'You're right there, Frank,' I agreed quietly.

We headed into our own room and just lay on the bed, exhausted. We kissed goodnight, Frank put his arm around me and it felt as though we'd hardly been asleep any time at all when it was six o'clock and breakfast was ready. We weren't that hungry but we ate anyway.

Michael said he should get us back to the farm before it was too bright. We shook hands with all the others and then went out through the big doors and drove away. We hadn't much to say to each other that morning because the four of us were tired. After about an hour or so we arrived at the farmhouse. Frank got out and opened the gate and Michael turned the car.

'We won't delay,' he said. 'I will see you during the week and we will make another arrangement for you to meet

Angel and spend a day or a night with her. She is in good hands and very happy. But we'd better go.' So they went off.

As we walked towards our cottage, the farmer came running out.

'Well, well, well!' he was saying. His wife came after him and she had her morning coat on her. 'By the look of you, you are very tired.'

'That we are,' Frank told them. 'We are exhausted.'

'Well, you needn't do any work today. Come on in for breakfast first –'

'No, no,' Frank assured them. 'We're after getting breakfast and we're full.'

The pair of them were very excited, eager for news. You could see their eyes lighting up. But I felt that they knew there was something on our minds that wasn't there before. We went off up to our cottage. We didn't make tea or anything. We just took off our clothes and dived into bed and we didn't waken till five o'clock that evening. We got up then and had a wash. Frank had a shave and said, 'I better go out and do a few jobs.'

He went out to the yard to do little bits and pieces and then went down the field to have a look at the cattle and the sheep. I went down to the house.

'Listen, Molly,' the farmer's wife said to me. 'You needn't do this. Any time you want off, you are welcome to it. We do other work besides the farm – as you'll find out some day. So you needn't be grateful to us, 'tis we are grateful to you. God sent you to us like he does a lot of the people that we are helping. Helping you Molly, is helping the people's Cause. So don't be thinking you owe us anything. You are two fine people. When the time comes we will miss you and we'll always be wondering where you are and what you are doing. If you get to America, we'll know you're fine, but in this country we wouldn't know because we can't ask anyone. However, every day that goes by, you are winning the battle. We can see it.'

'Thanks very much,' I said. My heart was racing in my chest. 'We didn't think we were that important but now we are feeling a bit important because everyone says what you just said – that we're important to them and to the things they do for people.'

✳ *Chapter 14* ✳

*T*he farmer sat at the fire with his pipe and his book.

'Look at that fella over there,' his wife laughed aloud. 'He gets stuck in a book and he can't get out of it. He's reading about American history.'

'Ah, Angel has one of them books too,' I said.

'And where do you think he got it from? Michael and Mary. And he's stuck in it since he got it. He's trying to figure out what the Irish and the Americans had in common, if anything.'

With that Frank came in the door and told the farmer that everything was all right on the farm, the cattle bedded down and the horses fed and looked after.

'Sure I know that,' says the farmer to Frank. 'You're a better man than me at it. And another thing,' he says, putting the book down on his lap, 'for all your own troubles, you show great interest in the well-being of the farm and us. As Florence said to Molly, we are going to miss you when you go away. We know you have to move sometime but we'll be sorry to see you go.'

We were all quiet for a few minutes. Then the farmer stood up with his back to the fire and looked at me and began to talk again. 'You see, them police will be back shortly. They want you to move on, but I'm going to try to prolong your time here a bit longer. I'll see a doctor that I know and he'll vouch for me that I'm not well and that I need you for a few more months – well into the summer, anyway. He's a good man, the doctor, but as he often says, we have to tell lies to survive. People have to tell lies in this country. You have to pay everyone. You have to bribe to survive.'

He turned to Frank. 'I'm reading this book. It is the history of America and it says these people brought shiploads of slaves from Africa and places like that and sold them to the big estates in America. That they didn't know how to speak English and they didn't know why they were being badly treated and harassed. Terrible things were done to them.'

'Sure they were bought and sold like cattle,' says Frank.

'Oh yeah,' agreed the farmer, 'that's the way it was done over there. They were brought in in ships and sold to the big farms and the Big Houses. Servants to do all the dirty work that no one else would do. If they tried to escape, they would be hunted down like animals and brought back to the estate to be whipped to death in front of their friends to show them what would happen to them if they tried to escape. It is a very sad book. And as we are speaking, maybe Angel is reading the very same stuff because Mary bought her a book about American history too. I would say it'll make her wiser by the day. They interfered with the women and girls and they used them and humiliated them. What happened to you shows there is not much difference here now. It is a good job you can't read Frank, or you would maybe give up out of fear of what could happen to you all.'

He closed the book and put it on the table between us. 'I don't think I'll read much more of it myself because it is killing me inside to know the same is happening on our own doorstep where we all speak English and could rise up and do something about it. But there is nothing being done. Only for people like Tom and others in America who know the history of their grandparents, we couldn't hit back. We can't let another generation of people go through the same. But it is not happening fast enough for us and there's people dying as we speak. And they are not dying on the battlefield – they are dying on these estates and in the Big Houses that have them employed. They're dying of neglect, poverty and dampness in their homes. I'll tell you one thing

Frank, it is worth fighting for when you sit down and think about it.'

'I know,' Frank answered him. 'It's just that to protect my family I thought I was doing the right thing by keeping my mouth shut and going on about my work – doing three men's work sometimes.'

The farmer responded quickly and a bit angrily. 'The likes of you shouldn't have to do that! There is too much of that in this country. People bow to anybody with money. When you have no money, no one will listen and no one wants to know anything about you. That's why we do our bit – we're just a small cog in a big wheel, passing messages and sometimes helping people. The less anybody knows about us the better. There's lots like us up and down the land who believe in what the Brotherhood is doing and give a hand to the likes of you as well. It is the Americans coming over here – that's the only hope we have. Get aid from America and get our people away out of this country. The slaves had no escape; they could be hanged or shot. But when our people escape over there, they are twice as strong and more determined than ever to get their own back.

'So what I am trying to say to you Frank, is that it is a big Cause and not only for you. We must not be found out. A dead hero is a lost hero. You can't do any more for your country if you are dead. Keep alive and keep out of trouble and hit back in other ways.'

The farmer's wife turned round now and said, 'I think it is time you two men retired. I don't want you reading that book. It is upsetting you and winding you up. What I read in those books destroys my hopes, so I hope Angel doesn't take it too serious. Just leave it be. Say goodnight and see what tomorrow brings.'

'Ah sure I'm sorry if I was going on too much about it,' replied her husband.

'No, no,' I interrupted, half afraid they might argue or something. 'All this gives us lots to think about. "Better the devil you know" isn't always right. So long as we can hear and see, we'll be able to manage.'

'The difference is,' the farmer said back to me, 'if you go to America you will be with friends. You'll meet a lot of people like yourselves who got away. We'll go to bed. Tomorrow is another day.'

Frank and me said goodnight and headed back up to our cottage. We stayed sitting up in bed talking about the book.

'I didn't want to say anything,' said Frank, 'but I didn't want to hear a lot of that. I feel bad now. Angel is in the middle of it all. What the farmer was telling us happened to the slave women and their daughters: that's exactly what we ran away from. So long as Angel is safe, let it be. We'll see what tomorrow brings.'

We didn't hear or see anyone until the end of the following

week. A car came up the road and we knew it was the Sweeneys. It pulled into the yard and Michael and Mary got out of the car.

'Open that back door!' Michael called out. 'I want to show you something.'

So Frank opened the door and there on the back seat was a shawl with a big lump under it.

'Pull that shawl off there.'

So Frank pulled the shawl off only to find Angel covered up in the back! She let out a big scream and jumped from the car to hug us and kiss us. She was laughing and excited by the idea of hiding on us in the car. The farmer and his wife gave her a great welcome too, hugging her and kissing her. We went into the house and Angel told us everything she had been doing. I was hoping she wouldn't mention the book and she didn't. We had a big tea then.

It was a great day. Angel walked round the farm to see her favourite animals – the horse and the pony, the sheep and lambs. Back at the cottage, we sat down to chat. Angel went down to her room and was there alone for a while. When she came out, the tears were still in her eyes and I asked, 'What's wrong, Angel?'

'Isn't it shocking I can't stay with you? I'm lonesome for you and afraid every day that goes by that someone will come in, recognise me and take me away altogether.'

'Angel, no one will do that. You're with good people.'

'I read a book on America,' she says, 'about the black people and slaves. It was like it was us they were talking about, only worse. I've never seen a black person but I can imagine what they went through.'

'You'll have to stop reading all that,' I told her.

'But Mam,' she says, 'I've got to tell you.'

'I've heard it all, Angel. I'd sooner you'd put that book away till such time as you see things in a different light and not be upsetting yourself. You are going to be safe and free. You won't need to be afraid of anyone again. Don't be reading that book – promise me you won't think about it any more. We have to be in the best of form for all those people who are trying to help us escape our situation.'

'But we got away,' says Angel. 'You and Dad saved me from what happened to them women in America.'

'I know that, Angel. Read something else. Read something with joy in it. Not sorrow and hardship and rape and murder and other things you shouldn't be reading at your age.'

'OK, Mam,' she says without any resistance. 'I won't read any more of it. I won't let you down for you never let me down. I'll put the book away.'

I went back to the farmyard and told Mary all about Angel and the book.

'Oh Molly,' she says, 'I was so sorry I gave that book to Angel.' Then she added, 'I was sorrier for giving it to the farmer. I thought everything here was perfect, you know. Since then my whole attitude has changed towards Ireland …'

We went on down the lane. Mary wanted to see the wild flowers in the ditches. Frank was in front of us with Michael. I asked Mary if there was any news yet.

'Well, don't raise your hopes but there is news. Tom got to his destinations and he is getting on well. It should only be a matter of weeks before he's back with word for you of what is happening up in your county.'

'That's great news Mary.'

'But,' she went on, 'again, don't bank on it. Michael is handling all that. Don't get too excited for it mightn't happen for a month. I'd say Michael is telling Frank anyway. These men only talk to men.' And she laughed. 'They like to get in there first. After all it is them who are putting their necks on the block. All we have to do is to keep our mouths shut and back them up and give them a bit of comfort when they are down and look after them like good wives. So I wouldn't say anything to Frank. Men are very funny. They can explode at one little thing and if they don't feel like talking they don't talk. They always have a lot on their minds, Molly.'

'Oh, I know that Mary. Me and Frank work together in fact, and you know it is very hard not to bring things up the odd time.'

'But you just have to wait this out,' she said.

We went back up the laneway towards the farm where we could see Angel and the farmer and his wife walking the paddock where they kept the horses. Angel was linking the two of them.

'Look at that,' said Mary. 'Isn't she so friendly? They love her. That's something to be proud of – she still has kindness in her heart after all that's happened. She is going to be a great woman some day as I told you Molly, and there's the proof of it. And everyone in the hotel loves her. Her manner is the best I have ever seen in any young person and I've taught in schools so I know young people inside out. Once she gets out of this country, she is going to do very well. So will you and Frank when you come to America.'

'Well, you say Mary, when we come to America …'

'I'm very optimistic and I know there is a lot being done to get you out because we need you over there to help us. You may think you're not educated but you can talk and you can tell people at meetings what's really happening here. You see, people have to be convinced Molly, and talked to, before they can decide what kind of aid they are going to give or what they might do to help the people here. We have to have people to talk to them and I think you and Frank could be the best ambassadors this country has to tell the stories. No one knows better than you two. I am very confident that you will do very well and so will Angel. 'Tis hard to know yet whether you're able to go to America or not. We extended our holiday to see if the four of us and Angel could board the same ship. That would be a victory for everyone.'

Soon after we reached the farm, the men appeared and Michael remarked, 'You must have had a good old chat? You look very happy there together.'

'Oh we did, Michael,' I told him. 'We had a good old laugh.'

We didn't tell him what we were discussing because we didn't want them to feel like we were interfering with their business.

Frank seemed a bit brighter than he had earlier that morning and I said to him, 'Well, had you a good chat, your-self and Michael? You talk about us women gabbing. You are worse than we ever were!'

Frank started laughing. 'We were only talking about the weather and the scenery. And I think I know what you two were going on about – paints and powders and scents and all that business!'

And there was a big laugh between the four of us. The farmer walked down the yard with his wife. Angel was between them, an arm around each of them. The wife called out to us, 'Time for tea, everyone. It's getting cold and Angel has to get back – she's working tonight. There's a big party and she has to be there. You know, we miss her around the place.'

'It keeps us going to know that you all love her,' I said to everyone. 'It keeps me and Frank happy knowing you look after her.'

'That's good,' says Michael. 'I'll bring her back again. But I hope she won't have to hide much longer.'

We watched the car until it went out of sight. We didn't speak. We just leaned across the gate watching. We went back and thanked the farmer for the welcome they'd given Angel.

'We don't need any thanks. Angel thanked us herself by coming here. Now,' says the farmer, 'we'll retire to our bed. I want you to get the pony and trap ready for me in the morning. Me and the missus are going to the town on a bit of business. We'll probably be gone all day and if it gets too late and is dark we'll stay in Sweeney's hotel for the night and be back in the morning. You and Molly know what's to be done. I don't have to tell you.'

'Oh yes,' says Frank. 'Stay as long you want and have a break.'

'No, no. It's not a break,' said the farmer. 'It's just something I have to do …'

We went back up to the cottage and lit the fire. We didn't know what to say to one another. It was dragging out on us, the whole thing.

Molly stopped her tale for a moment and looked at me curiously. 'Just like the way this story is dragging out on you, Pat.'

But I told her, and Frank too, 'Molly, I don't mind. Just tell me everything and don't think about how I feel. I'll tell you if I want you to stop.'

'Thanks, Pat,' she said, 'it's great to know that you are listening to everything that I have to say. But it is a long story and if you are fed up just tell me that you've had enough of it.'

'I'm definitely not giving up and I don't want you to give up,' I said. 'I'm your friend and I hope that you are my friends, so tell me everything. Then I can tell it to people just like you're telling it to me.'

'Thanks very much Pat,' Molly smiled at me. 'I'll carry on from the next day ...'

✳ *Chapter 15* ✳

*W*e got up the next day and got the pony and trap ready for the farmer and his wife and off they went, all dressed up, down the lane. We carried on with our usual work. We hadn't much to say to each other all day because Angel's visit knocked the stuffing out of us. We couldn't believe just how beautiful and grown-up she was getting every time we saw her. So, you can understand how we felt that night and the next day; we were just in a very bad mood. But not really with each other.

We didn't know why the farmer and his wife had gone into town. We'd never ask because they went in occasionally to get provisions. Because they lived so far from town, they would have to get extra stuff in and they'd always bring us something. The farmer's wife would get me something to wear or the farmer would get Frank cigarettes and tobacco. It just felt like we were related to them.

Late that evening I was in the house, dusting and cleaning and keeping the fire going. Frank was outside finishing up the few jobs and keeping an eye out for them.

'I don't think they're coming home tonight Molly,' he said when he came in. 'I think we'd better stay here the night and get up early and have things ready and the fires lit.'

I didn't feel comfortable staying in their house like that, even though it was what they always wanted when they were away. I made the supper for Frank and we stayed up talking.

Next morning, at half-seven, Frank went off about his jobs. He'd never take breakfast until nine. I got up, lit the fires and put on the breakfast. After breakfast Frank went down the yard and I went outside to hang out the washing. I looked down the laneway and I could see this figure of a man. He was at least six-foot tall. It was a very foggy morning and I didn't know whether it was a policeman or what, so I called Frank.

'There's someone coming up the lane – maybe it's a policeman …'

'Right,' says Frank. 'Go on into the house and I'll stand around the gate and wait.'

I watched out the window. Frank had a brush and he was sweeping round the gate and letting on he was busy but he had his eye fixed on the laneway. This big man with a satchel on his back came up to the gate and started talking to Frank. They were shaking hands so I guessed he must be a friend of the farmer. They came on into the house.

'Molly,' Frank asked, 'will you put on some breakfast for this man? He's after coming a long, long way to see the farmer. He's a friend. He knows them and the Sweeneys and Michael and Mary.'

'I know everything and I know everyone,' the man said, laughing. 'I am tired indeed and could do with a bit to eat. And my clothes are wet and I would like to lie down. I'm on the go for weeks,' he said, 'and I haven't seen anyone or talked to anyone since the last farmhouse I was in miles back the road. I have to see Pearse and Florence. I have messages for them.'

I fed him and told him to throw his clothes outside the door before he went to bed and I would wash them and dry them at the fire for him. So he did that and I washed the clothes and hung them out for a while and then brought them in and put them round the fire to dry. I ironed his shirt and trousers to have everything ready for when he'd get up.

Frank went off about his jobs and came back after about two hours saying, 'The pony and trap is on the way up. I can see it in the distance. The fog's lifted.'

He went down and opened the gate. I could see the farmer and his wife from the window. I had the kettle boiled and was dying to hear their news.

Frank went out to tell them about the man who had come with a message who wanted to wait for them to get back. I went outside to meet them. The farmer's wife wrapped her arms around me and said that she enjoyed her bit of time away from the farm. I told her that we missed them.

'Oh, we missed you too,' she said. 'There's no place like home. No matter what you have or haven't, it's a grand thing to have your own place away from all the troubles of the world.'

'Ah, that's right,' I said back to her. 'We feel the same. We feel at home here.'

'And you'll be at home here for another while anyway. The boss will tell you all about it. We'll go in.'

They had had breakfast in Sweeney's hotel and weren't hungry but we all had a cup of tea.

'Let that man sleep,' she said.

The farmer spoke to Frank. 'I'm very sorry Frank, I should have told you. I was expecting this man a week ago. He had a bit of a problem getting through. He goes by the name of Bill and that is all you need to know. He's a friend of a friend of mine and he was here before.'

'Oh,' said Frank with a smile, 'he knew his way to the room, anyway!'

The farmer laughed. 'Yes, he does and all. He is one of our own and he brings the news to people round here. I think you gather that now, don't you, Frank?'

'I do,' said Frank. 'Just doing their job.'

'Exactly,' said the farmer.

I told the farmer that he could do with a rest.

'I got too much rest! But I want to tell you something, Frank.' He laughed and punched the table with his fist. 'I got six months of an extension for you. I was with the doctor and I was down in the police station. What delayed us was the sergeant wasn't there. I had to wait until he came in the next morning to nearly beg him to let you two stay. I had the doctor's note and gave it to him and he says, "I give him six months more to help you out." After that I have to go in again and if you are not gone in six months he is going to investigate who you are and why you're not moving on. But at least I have the doctor's note and they can't do very much to me. But he can harass me. They can come every other day to see am I working or if I need the help. I didn't push it.'

'That's great,' Frank said delightedly. 'That is great news.'

'You'd be here for a lot longer if I had my way. You would be here for good. But they don't want to see you settling down or anything. At least you are all right for now. When you go, I'll just say you disappeared one morning or something and they'll be happy. So they will think there was no love lost between us. They love to hear us running the workers down. Isn't it an awful thing to have to run down your friends for them to stay out of jail, but what can we do? What they don't know can't bother them! You and Molly go on back up to the cottage. I want to have a chat with Bill when he wakens. He can't stay very long – a few days at the most – and we have a lot to discuss. Michael and Mary will be out tomorrow or the day after because they want to meet Bill too. I have to get word in to them that he is here. Thanks for looking after the place.'

'There's no need to thank me,' said Frank. 'I feel like I'm almost part of the family now.'

'Indeed you are, Frank. You and Molly. Like brothers and sisters. Come back down for supper to have a chat with Bill.'

So we went off. 'The less that knows our business the better and the less we know, the better for our own good,' I said to Frank. 'There's something going on and I hope it's good.'

'That's what I'm thinking too,' Frank agreed. 'But I'm not getting my hopes up. And I don't want you to get your hopes up too much. I don't want to see you crying again. You've had enough. More than any woman could stick and you're still on the go.'

'And so are you, Frank. We're two of a kind. If God made us, he matched us!'

Frank laughed. 'Yeah, if God made us, he matched us right.'

Later in the evening Frank went out, milking the cows and feeding the calves. 'I'll come back then and shave and get dressed and we'll wait till the farmer calls us.'

'But he said to come down, Frank,' I told him.

'Well, I won't nor neither will you. We'll wait here till he calls. I don't want to walk in on their conversation. The farmer will know why we're not down. Bill was very tired, Molly, worn out like us when we were being put through the mill.'

'I'm coming out to give you a hand,' I said.

'Right,' says Frank. 'Come on. I'll give you plenty to do.' Frank milked the cows and I fed the calves and the pigs. It took us about two hours to finish the jobs. Then we went in and washed ourselves and put on our clean clothes and sat there talking. Next thing, a rap came on the door.

'I thought I told you to come down,' the farmer said.

'Ah,' said Frank, 'I didn't want to come down in case we might break up your conversation.'

'Well,' says he, 'I should have known. Come on down now. Our talk is done. I'll introduce you to Bill.'

On the way down the yard together, he praised everything. The yard was clean and the sheds were clean. He never checked up on us for he knew well it'd be done. We went into the house.

'Now, we only go on first names round here you know, Frank. This is Bill,' the farmer said. 'He's from near your country. A few miles only. He travels from county to county and town to town with news for us.'

'I understand,' Frank replied.

'Well,' says this Bill to us, 'I can't say very much to you and Molly. Pearse and Michael and Mary will fill you in on what's being done. But just to take the agony out of it, I can tell you this much. I met Tom. Your friend the blacksmith is alive and well. And his wife. Getting on with business. Everything is the same as it was when you left. Things don't change up there. They were asking for you and said they were praying for you. Tom said he'll be in contact very shortly. That things are moving faster than he expected. He said to tell you not to worry and to keep your heads up and keep the faith and everything will work out. So that's it for now. And thanks – you made a good job of my clothes and I feel great now again. I told Pearse I drank some of his whiskey.'

'Frank is very generous with my whiskey, you know,' the farmer laughed as he got the bottle out again …

'Molly,' I interrupted her, 'would you not be afraid of letting in a total stranger like him and dealing with him?'

She answered without hesitation. 'When you're as long on the road as we were and deal with the people that we met, you get to know by their eyes and their tone of voice. You learn the hard way. Their eyes tell you the story and you know if you have a friend or an enemy. That's how we learned to judge people, Pat.'

'All right, Molly, I see what you mean. Sorry for interrupting. Just carry on again …'

So she told me that the man Bill looked tired. That he was very drawn in the face and the few drinks were going to his head because he wasn't used to it. He was like ourselves, she said.

The farmer was happy enough: 'I heard what I wanted to hear and everything is going well and as Bill told you, Tom is doing his stuff. He's a saint.'

'He's a real good man,' his wife added. 'I wouldn't be worried any more now.'

'That's the best news that we heard in a long time. There must have been someone praying for us, for us to come to here and get such good treatment,' I said.

'Oh, go away with that,' the farmer answered me quickly. 'Look at the treatment I'm getting from you. I hadn't to do a tap of work since you came. I won't know how to work when you leave.'

'You have nothing to worry about,' Bill assured us. 'Michael and Mary, Tom, Pearse and Florence here will settle everything. You've been through an awful lot but you're not showing much sign of it. You're good strong people and that's what this country needs, strong people with strong minds and a will to live. It's people like you who will make this country worth living in and fighting for. People who go through the mill and can tell the truth. There is no good in forgetting about it when you go down the road. There will be others coming behind who need education and peace and jobs for their families. That's why I'm here tonight; I'm just spreading the word. God is good and things will work out for you. Whether it is here or America, you'll find a way to live in peace. So I'll say goodnight now. I'm off to bed again. You might think I'm lazy but I'm dead tired,' he laughed.

The farmer turned to Frank. 'You and Molly have a lie-in in the morning and I'll do the few jobs and the missus will do the housework. Have a bit of a rest.'

'Oh, no,' I insisted. 'Me and Frank will do the work in the morning and leave you two to have a bit of a sleep-in. You're doing us the good turn. We'll do the work. It keeps our minds off other things.'

'All right,' says the farmer, 'sure you have us spoiled rotten. We're like two children here we're so spoiled, me and the missus.'

Bill laughed. 'It's not everyone would do that for you.'

'Who are you telling?' laughed the farmer. 'You'd have to beat some up out of bed to get them up to do anything!'

The morning came fairly quickly. Frank went out on the farm. I washed the delft and did my cleaning and polishing. The farmer's wife got up at half-nine and the farmer soon after.

'Good God!' he says. 'You have everything done, Molly.'

'Your breakfast is there in the oven and Bill's is ready if he's up,' I said.

The door opened behind me and Bill comes in and says, 'I am up, Molly. I smelled your fry and I'm starving.'

The farmer asked me to call Frank in for his breakfast. The way it was with Frank he didn't like going in to eat when there was anyone there in the house, but the farmer wouldn't hear tell of him standing out there or waiting around till they were finished. 'We'll sit together in this house. We won't make fish of one and flesh of the other,' he said. So I called Frank in and you'd know by his face that he felt a bit embarrassed.

'What news?' the farmer's wife asked about the animals.

'Ah,' says Frank, 'you've a new calf this morning and you've two new lambs and I think the pig is going to have young ones any time. We'll have to split it between us to sit up with her.'

'Great news! Life on the farm,' said the farmer. 'This is what makes farming worth the effort. To see the new life coming. I love this time of the year.'

'And so do I,' Frank told everyone. 'I worked on farms from eight years old.'

'I could tell that,' the farmer says, 'by the way that you are able to manage. You could run a place ten times as big.'

'Don't be giving me a swelled head now,' laughed Frank, 'or my cap won't fit me going out.'

We were all having a good laugh at that when we heard a

car coming in. The farmer told Frank to go out and see who it was.

'Tell me who it is. I don't want to be seen outside if it is the police or anything like that coming to see if I am in bed. They'll have to see I amn't able to get out and work …'

Frank came back in immediately. 'It's Mary and Michael.'

'Great!' said the farmer. He turned to Bill. 'They're here.'

'Thank God,' said Bill, sounding relieved. 'I think I should be shifting on. I'm glad that I don't have to wait another day, not but that I'm spoiled here with Molly and Frank and you two. Sure who wants to leave this place?'

Frank and I went out to greet Michael and Mary.

'Is Bill here?' they called out.

'He's waiting to see the two of you,' Frank told them.

'Great. We didn't think he'd be here. We heard he might be delayed.'

They went on into the house. We went up to our cottage to keep out of the way and not to be seen listening to what they were saying. They could be very secretive at times.

✳ *Chapter 16* ✳

*W*e often heard everything that went on, all their talk and business, but half the time we didn't understand what they were saying. We were happy enough that they weren't saying bad things about us and we'd keep our noses out of their business. When they'd want us to know something, they'd tell us. But they weren't overloading our minds. They were overloaded themselves; they looked so worried at times. They'd be hours and hours talking. It was never just for five minutes. When they'd call us, we'd come in to hear what they wanted to tell us.

A few hours went by and me and Frank were in the cottage, and in comes Mary, her usual happy self.

'I've word from Angel for you that's she's doing well and hopes you are keeping all right and not missing her too much. And by the way Frank, the men want to have a talk with you down below. I'll sit here with Molly. We can't stay much longer because Bill has to be on his way. We're taking him in the car.'

Frank went off and after about an hour came up to tell us they were all ready to leave. So we walked Mary down to the car where Bill said to me, 'Molly, thanks very much for all you did for me, and thanks Frank, for the chat and please God, we might meet again one day for a jar.'

Michael turned round to me and said, 'I'm very sorry, Molly, that I hadn't much time to talk to you this evening but I'll be talking to you at length soon. I've to get Bill well away from here to go about his business. Frank will fill you in on some of the things that we told him. Don't be worried. We'll sort the whole thing out.'

We said our goodbyes and off they went. We went in and the farmer's wife made the tea while the farmer spoke to us. 'As Bill told you, everything is going well for Tom. He met Donoghue the blacksmith and his wife, and is getting some help from them. We have to wait and see how he gets on in the parish church. It's only a matter of a few days or a week at the most until Tom has his research completed. The situation above in Meath is not easy. Your posters are still outside the station and on the post office and town hall and all. The reward is still there. So they are not giving up trying to find you. This is what is worrying Tom in case the least bit of suspicion arises and he gets caught. But he is doing well with his tourist act anyway. He's getting away with it so far. He can't stay away from his parish in America very long either or they might start asking questions over there. There are some people there who wouldn't be very happy with what he is doing. There is great sympathy for you from everyone he has spoken to and from your friends that he met. They all wanted to know whether you were alive or dead. Tom told them you were alive but wouldn't tell them where you were, just in case. I am expecting Michael and Mary to come early next week with some sort of word for us. So don't get downhearted. Your friends are alive and kicking and so are you.'

'Thanks,' said Frank. 'I'm glad Ned Donoghue and his wife are well and remember us. Some day we'll make it up to them for the help they are giving. It's not everyone would take the chance to help people like us. People are either too afraid or too loyal to the landlords to risk anything for you. It's friends like the blacksmith and his wife who come good.'

It was getting late so we went back up to the cottage and went to bed. After about an hour and a half, I whispered, 'Are you awake, Frank?'

'I am, Molly.'

'I can't sleep.'

'Neither can I. The waiting and wondering about what is happening keeps me up.'

'I think I'll get up and make a cup of tea.'

I was up in the kitchen, a little fire lit up, a small kettle of water on, when Frank got up too. He had his trousers on him and his jumper. He says, 'Look Molly, it's ridiculous going to bed. I just can't handle it. I tried to sleep and I twisted and turned and thought you were asleep. You know the way we are anyway …'

The kettle boiled and we drank a pot of tea between us. It was coming to morning, about half-four or five. We sat on the old couch and we fell asleep in our clothes. The alarm clock went off at half-seven and sure we had to get up again to do the work. Frank went off to do his business and I went down to the farmhouse and tidied up from the night before and got the fire lit and started up breakfast. The farmer's wife got up.

'Molly,' she said to me, 'you look terrible this morning. Your eyes are red. You're very white in the face and you don't look well.'

'Me and Frank were up all night. We couldn't sleep till coming on morning. We just can't seem to get it into our heads that things are being done for us. The wait and the terror is still in us. Every day that goes by it seems to be getting longer. And I'm afraid for Frank. He's the strongest man of the whole lot and carrying me with him. But I feel myself getting weary and tired and disappointed with myself. I'm trying to keep him going. If he breaks I'm gone too and so is Angel. I know you do your best but I'm just not able to cope. I can't explain it. We feel even more isolated now that things are coming to a head and worry that some day soon a wrong decision could be made and after that nothing could be done for us. That would really kill us. We don't want to be a burden on you and your husband. Frank won't give in but he might just turn round some day and say, "I'll take to the roads again and see if we can do more than we are doing now." That's what I'm dreading. I'm trying to keep him going, and myself too, but I'm losing the battle.'

At that the farmer walked in from the parlour. 'I heard all that, Molly,' he said. 'I know how you feel. I can see the strain in your faces. We didn't sleep a wink last night either. We're trying to keep you going but it is also the other way round – you are keeping us going. I want to make you a promise: I am going to step things up. You've waited long enough for some sort of answer and now I am going to do something about it. Go on out, Molly,' he said. 'Bring Frank in. Tell him to drop whatever he's doing and come down to the house. I want to have a few words with him.'

So I went up the yard where Frank was coming out of one of the sheds and I shouted out at him to come down to the house.

'What's wrong?' he asked as we all sat around the table.

'Things are not happening fast enough,' the farmer told him, without mentioning what I had said to them. 'Frank, you're very tired-looking.'

'Ah, there's not a bother on me,' says Frank, keeping the good side out.

'I am going to send for Joe Sweeney to step this up and see if something can be done in the next week or so. I'm like yourselves, waiting for word. I'm thinking of Angel too and what would happen if you had to go off in the morning. You'd still have to leave her behind. You couldn't bring her on the road again. If there is nothing soon, I can arrange something for you in a different part of the country. But, as you know yourselves, it won't be any different. Whatever about being a change, it is going to be no different. There is plenty of Ireland worse off than Meath, Dublin or any other of these counties. There is no hiding place but I don't want you going off again without a destination, just travelling around. You could end up in the wrong place to work and somebody would suddenly be claiming that reward. They'd make you say where Angel was. I'm telling you there is no easy hiding place in Ireland for people who run away from these big estates.'

'I have faith in you,' Frank said to him. 'And we're not giving up.'

His wife sat there speechless at the farmer's long outburst.

Frank suspected that they must have heard something that didn't go down well with them. He didn't know that it was me telling them how I felt and what I was afraid of. I kept that to myself and put a brave face on things.

'But I'll tell you one thing, Pat...' Molly paused for a minute, looking at me, I suppose, to see if I was taking it all in. She seemed to want to explain herself to me. 'I was losing it fast.' She nodded to herself at the memory. 'Every time I'd look at Frank and his hands cracked from the weather and his face white for the want of sleep – I woke up several nights and he'd let on he was asleep but I knew he wasn't. Even when he had a few drinks in him he would stay awake as well.' She patted Frank on the knee.

'We were watching each other to see which of us was going to break and both of us tried to keep the other going. But I felt like I was the weakest link in this because of the loss of my children. As a mother, it went through my heart. I was thinking of them more each day that went by. My three boys lying in a cold grave in a very lonely churchyard in Meath.

'Frank knew what I was thinking – he missed them too; they were his sons and he loved them. I'd never really ask Frank was he about to give up because we were afraid in case we might come to a decision to give ourselves up and go back and face jail. But we weren't going to let Angel down. If we were going to get caught, it would happen back near the estate where we worked,

not around Cork or with any of the people who helped us along the way. We'd make sure that we were caught back in Meath. This was all going through my mind. So you know how I felt. Talking about all this is really getting me down now and look at Frank here – he doesn't say very much because he is just not able to handle it any more.'

Molly paused for a long time, and the tent was silent with sadness.

'Keep going, Molly,' Frank eventually said quietly, and he looked over at me. 'Pat will remember every word you tell him.'

'I will, I will without doubt,' I said passionately, their emotions filling me up too. And I meant it.

'Will you go up and put the pony in the trap?' the farmer asked Frank a few days later. 'I'm going off for a day or two, or maybe three.' He was full of energy. He had the look of a man whose blood was boiling and I immediately had the feeling that he was going to do something he shouldn't.

'I hope you are not going to get yourself into trouble,' I said. 'We've been avoiding that all these years. Me or Frank don't want to get you into any trouble.'

'Molly, let me handle it. I'll have something when I am coming up that road again. I was being too optimistic that things were going right. I want you and Frank to move into the house until I come back. What I'm going to do I can't do sitting here. The best thing is to go into town. I can do a lot of stuff for myself as well as helping you. Maybe I got too comfortable waiting for people to come to me when I should be going to them. They're afraid of being seen coming up here too often. On my own I can move around and get to see people that have some sort of push and pull.'

Frank came with the pony and trap.

'I'll be back whenever I am ready,' the farmer said to us, and away he went, trotting down the lane.

I told Frank the whole story then.

'But we don't want him to get into trouble over us or Angel so I hope he doesn't do anything foolish,' he said.

'Not at all,' said the farmer's wife. 'He has a good name. They know him all over the country, they do. But as you see, you are being watched and the my husband is also being watched closely. They say good morning or good evening when they meet on the street – even the police do. But they keep an eye on him. They know there is something going down with him but they are not sure. If they got anything on him they'd be very happy to jail him. We'll talk about something else for the next few days. To take your minds off the worries. We'll try, anyway.'

And she got up off her chair and she went over to the kettle and she took out her bottle of whiskey. 'Molly, did you ever drink a hot whiskey?'

'No,' says I. 'I never touched whiskey. It's only the sherry I drank.'

'You'll like this!' she laughed. 'I'm going to make a jug of punch and we're going to have a drink before bed.'

So she made a big jug of punch as she called it. With sugar and cloves in it. I never tasted anything like it. Lovely it was! We drank the full jug between the three of us and she jumped up and made another one. Between the talking and the laughing, we forgot about the world outside. We finished the second jug and we were a bit tipsy.

'Now,' she announced, 'there's a fire lit in the spare room and when you wake in the morning have a bit of a lie-in. I'll give you a hand out, Molly. Or maybe the two of us will go out and give Frank a hand before breakfast.'

We didn't wake until half-nine the next morning and neither did the farmer's wife. So I got up in a kind of a panic, for the day is short enough in the wintertime without sleeping-in in the mornings. I lit the fire and called Frank. The farmer's wife must have heard me up in the kitchen. She got up and she burst out laughing when she saw me. 'Aren't we right ones, sleeping to nearly ten o'clock in the morning and a farm to be run!'

We had a good laugh about the night before. 'We should do that every night.' she said, doing a bit of a swing around the floor.

'Oh, I couldn't do that,' I said. 'We'd never get up for work again and we'd all be alcoholics!' We were laughing about it all day.

After a couple of days we started wondering about how the farmer was getting on. You'd know by the farmer's wife's eyes that she was getting anxious. Four more days went by. But on the Sunday morning, the trap came back up the laneway. We nearly jumped for joy, we were so pleased to see him. It seemed like ages since he had left. He was smiling as always. He was generally a good-humoured man and rarely showed his feelings, and that night at the table with his wife we saw the first bit of emotion from him in all the time we worked there.

'Come on in,' the farmer said. 'I have something to tell you.'

We had our fingers crossed. Me and Frank looked at one another as if to say, Oh my God, what's the word on us and Angel? Is he going to tell us something that will break our hearts or what? His wife had the tea on – the minute she saw him coming she had the kettle boiling. He had a big mug he always drank out of and it was on the table the whole time he was gone. He loved this mug that his wife bought him for his birthday years ago.

'Well,' he began, 'I don't regret that I went off. Just listen to me and try and take in what I am saying. I got in contact with Tom through friends. Now the man from the registry office in Cork here, he can't do anything. He can do nothing about the registry. He can't register any of you, either you, Frank or Angel ...'

We felt something coming on and we looked at one another and waited for him to continue.

'Once we knew your background and that none of you were registered we could move forward. But Tom wasn't sure because he had no one to enquire about your details. I said that he would find that the big estate had already been checking for your registration details to see exactly who you were and to have a proper profile on you for the police.

'Tom wants to talk to you in person, along with Mary and Michael. The best thing to do is to leave it at that. I saw Angel nearly every morning and sometimes in the evening. She is happy and has friends to go out and about with – you know the way they like to walk round together having a chat. She is getting more like a young woman every day. She told me to tell you that she misses you, and she misses the farm too. But still she is happy where she is. She'll see us as soon as she has time off, if Mary and Michael or even Joe Sweeney can bring her out. I think the time is getting short. So come on and join me in a little drink for my return. Anyway, you two are staying down here for a few nights more. That'll stop me and the wife from fighting with each other!'

We all laughed at that and the farmer's wife got the bottle and held it up. 'A little drink of what?' she said. 'It's gone!'

'Come off it. You didn't drink all my whiskey?!'

'Every drop,' I said, laughing along with his wife.

'I've got a few hid away, so don't worry. I've them hid from you,' he added, looking at his wife.

'And I was thinking that you were making a whole lot of visits up to the hay barn,' she responded.

I knew they wanted to have a talk. 'If you don't mind,' I said, 'me and Frank will go into the parlour for a while.' We knew that Father Tom now had something final and we could do whatever we liked after that. That was something we had to talk about. And we could sense that Angel would be all right. I could see a new light ahead. Fair play to the farmer. So we went into the parlour and stayed there until it was late. We'd had a few more hot whiskeys, so we had a good night's sleep.

The farmer slept on late next morning. He might have looked tired but he was very happy. We think he did some of his own business as well as ours. It took a weight off all our minds to know there was some news on the way. It was a great feeling. The days and nights didn't seem as long. That was a real sign – that we were happy and rested. It was a great suggestion the farmer had made for us to move in to the house because we felt like we were part of a family again.

'I have a lot of stories to tell but I won't tell you now and I might never tell you but you know that I am doing my best to help you,' the farmer would say.

'Oh, we know,' Frank would answer. 'But you are not

to overdo it. You're being very kind to people not used to kindness. So I hope you know what we think and that we won't blame you for anything that goes wrong. You have done your best and that is all that you can do. I'll help you out as much as I can and when I can, and anything I can do to help you with your own work I'll do it,' says Frank.

'Spoken like a true Irishman!' laughed the farmer.

❋ *Chapter 17* ❋

*O*ne day a car came up the road. We hadn't seen this car before. So we told the farmer and went about our work. The well-dressed gentlemen who got out shook hands with the farmer and when his wife came out, she put her arms around him and they embraced for a long time.

I was watching out the window at all this going on and Frank could see it all as well from the shed. This person was no stranger. The car was big. We had never seen it even around the town – but we weren't out much because we had to keep a low profile. They were being very friendly to one another and I didn't know what to think.

The farmer's wife shouted, 'Come down here, Molly. I want to introduce you to somebody.'

I went down. 'Molly, this is my brother Jack,' she says. 'He is working in a government office in Dublin and I don't see him very often. He is a bit of a Jack the Lad but he comes off and on to see us and he brought Tom back with him from Dublin! Tom will see you the day after tomorrow.'

I felt myself getting light in the head with excitement, or was it a weakness coming on from being over-anxious to know just what was going on? I gave Frank a shout to come down.

'Molly,' the brother says, 'I heard so much about you. No one knows what I do or no one wants to know probably.' And he laughed. 'But I know all about you and I have seen the posters and Tom filled me in on the rest and I talked with the blacksmith and his wife as well. I brought Tom around to different places. You have nothing to worry about, Tom told me to tell you. All should be solved within a few weeks if you are agreeable to what he is going to propose to you.'

'Oh, that's great,' I said to him, 'and thanks very much. I don't know what to say.'

'Well, just go out and bring that man of yours in till I shake the hand of him. I hear he is very brave, just like yourself,' he laughed. 'Strong willed, I hear.'

So I went out and I called Frank again. 'You needn't be

hiding. This is a friend. I'll let him introduce himself to you.'

Frank came in and Jack stood up from the table. 'You're Frank?'

'I am, and I believe,' says Frank, 'your name is Jack.'

'Well, I'm Florence's brother from Dublin. I heard a lot about you from Ned Donoghue and his wife, and Tom told me everything. Your tale really shocked me. To think these things can happen to people in this day and age. The time will come when those people will have to answer for what they've done.'

The farmer's wife prepared a meal and made us sit down with them. We talked for the best part of the day.

Frank eventually stood up. 'Now look, it is all right for you talking but I have work to do. I'm off out to the animals and I'm going to feel happy because I know Tom has something to tell us that you won't tell us.' He looked over at the farmer. 'You're too clever!'

There was more laughing. That's the way we used to carry on. You try and make a joke out of things. Anyway, Frank went out and I helped to clean up after the meal. It was time to go back up to the cottage, so I said to the farmer, 'Right, I'm going up to light the fire in the cottage and we'll stay there again for the night.'

I went into the cottage, tidied up, lit a little fire and got things going. Something really happened that morning. I could hear whistling coming from the yard. So I went outside and there was Frank whistling away. I hadn't heard him whistling in a long, long time. I felt so happy for him. Things were going back to the way they were years ago. To hear him whistle was a ray of hope for me.

Frank came in that evening and had a wash and sat down and we were talking in general about this, that and the other and what we were going to do when we heard another car pulling up in the yard. So we sneaked a look out the door, nosy as usual. It was Joe Sweeney. He was about half an hour or more in the house before he came up to our cottage. We let on we weren't watching him coming. He rapped on the door and Frank went out.

'How are you both?'

'Ah, we're doing all right.'

'I just came out to tell you that Angel hasn't a bother on her. She's learning all the tricks of the trade and is very happy with her new friends. She said to tell you she loves you and will see you soon – which she will. And another thing – tomorrow morning we are off very early with Jack. Jack is collecting me in his car and he is bringing the three of us on a long journey. About thirty miles from here. Michael and Mary will meet us there too. So at six o'clock in the morning be ready. You're going to meet Tom.'

'We're delighted, and thanks,' I said to Joe.

Joe went off down the yard and into his car and away home.

We woke about four the next morning. The farmer's wife had a big fry on for us. Jack was there with his suit on him, all well done up. After the breakfast he says, 'We'd better be off now. We don't want to be late. I have to collect Joe Sweeney.'

'I hope you win,' said the farmer, wishing us goodbye.

'And I say the same,' agreed the farmer's wife. 'I hope you do. I hope this will be the best day of your life and that God will turn round and do something for you.'

We all got into the car and away with us. There wasn't a soul on the roads or in the streets. We pulled up at the hotel and Joe came out with his case with him. 'Good morning,' he shouted with a smile, and he hopped into the car. We went miles and miles out the country, over back-roads and bad roads and good roads, places we had never been before. After nearly two hours we arrived at a nice old farmhouse, up a little road. A big farmer's house.

We pulled up by the door and a man came out. 'You're the people for Tom?' he said.

'Yes,' said Jack. 'We are.'

'You're welcome,' he said. 'Follow me.'

Father Tom was there with two others, and the man from the town registry office that the farmer had told us about. They looked all business-like as we came in. They had a tea for us.

'Did anything exciting happen while I was away?' Father Tom asked us with a smile.

'Ah no Father,' Frank said. 'But I think you know more about us than we know about you!' So there was a bit of a laugh at that, and Father Tom introduced us all.

'This is our friend from the registry office. These other two men – I'll not mention their names – they're friends of mine. One from Limerick and another from Kerry. And Michael and Mary are outside. I'll wait for them to come in before I tell you anything. Then we'll all discuss what's been happening and what I have in mind. If you agree with me, things can happen fast. Faster than you might think. But we have to wait and see what you think.'

Michael and Mary came in with their arms stretched out wide to greet us. They looked very tired as well.

Having told us how Angel was getting on, Michael said, 'We haven't much more time here. Whatever happens in the next couple of days, you and Frank will have to make your own minds up about what you want to do. Everything we tried came down to this conclusion. So just listen to us for a few minutes and you will have a few days to make your minds up and talk between yourselves. We all hope you make the right decision because we can't do that for you. Tom will tell you what's happening.'

We walked down a corridor with Father Tom to a room with chairs, a desk and all Father Tom's papers and his briefcase, as he called it. We sat down. Father Tom began his story.

'You know I've been up in Meath. I met Ned Donoghue and his wife and a couple of other people that knew you. The blacksmith's wife did a bit of research for me in the local church where Angel was supposed to be christened. She cleans the church as you know and helps out. She went over all the books in the vestry and there is no trace of Angel's name or of her being christened there. I've searched the registry myself. That's why the man from the registry office is here. He couldn't find anything to do with Angel or any of the rest of your family. There's nothing in the registry. That means that Angel no longer exists or, if you like, never existed officially either in the church or in the registry office under births, marriages and deaths. There is not even a death certificate for your three boys. So that means none of you exists officially.

'Now the thing about this is that if anyone looks you up they'll get nowhere. No one, not even our registry office friend here, can slip you on to the registry books now. You could go back to where each of you lived when you were single and you might be able to get some information. But if anybody looking for you hasn't got that information, and has you listed as Mr and Mrs Maguire from just outside Trim, they'll find nothing. What you are afraid of is Angel's situation. So now you needn't worry anymore because, as far as the official world is concerned, Angel never existed. And because of that, I have no problem bringing you all to

America. There are thousands of Irish over there who are not registered. But on the other hand, Angel has to go to school and college, and she will have to be registered in Ireland somehow.

'Now, this is the hardest part of my job. I don't know how you are going to feel about what I'm going to suggest but, if it were my decision, I would do it. Michael's son is coming out of the army and they have one child – a boy, Kevin. I know him well. I christened him. Michael Junior and his wife are willing to take on Angel. Although they have never met her, they are willing to do the necessary and go through all that has to be done to adopt the child. But the problem is that she can't be legally adopted because she isn't registered. So instead we will have to pretend that she was born to Michael Junior and his wife. There is no way to do that legally and officially, yet Angel must be made legal.

'So our proposal is that Mary here is her grandmother and Michael her grandfather. Michael Junior is moving to live in a new area where he is unknown so everyone will presume she is their daughter. It's an Irish community and they have closed mouths over there. No one says anything about anyone. So that's the proposal. Not for Michael Junior and his wife to adopt your daughter, Frank and Molly, but for them to pretend to be her natural parents. Now, I know and you know and we all know that Angel will never lose her true identity. She will always be your child. But to enable her to have a future in America this is the only way. I'll put her down as christened by me and I have a friend in the registry office in America who will put her down as being registered at an address in America. So she will be an American citizen. All the paperwork must be done very quickly because legislation is changing. The Irish come on the run to America and the Americans are beginning to notice what's happening and want to regulate it. Now you have to think about it. I know it can be organised because I have done all my homework. I have everything and everybody in place to help me out.'

He stopped for a moment for he could see that me and Frank wanted to get in and ask questions. But before we could open our mouths, he put up his hand and told us to wait until he had finished, and continued telling us about his proposal and how it would work out.

'We've even picked a name for Angel – Mary Jane O'Connell, daughter of Michael O'Connell Junior, et cetera, et cetera, you know what I mean. You can choose another name with her if you want to but this is the one we're suggesting. I'm also suggesting we christen Angel before she leaves this country. The way I see it, the child hasn't been christened. We can have a christening party here in this house and, if everything works out with yourself and Frank, we'll have one great day. We can't mention the name Angel here in Ireland but we will include it so that it will always be part of her name. What you decide is up to yourselves. It will be a hard decision to make – a terrible one even. Another misfortune for you really. But I can't see any other way out. Face the music here or face a new life in America.

'And that's it. I'm going to give you time to think it over. Whether it is a yes or a no, it is going to be very hard on you two. But we will all support your decision. We won't fight or argue over it.'

I turned to Frank and he looked at me in silence. The talk had gone on for ever and we were exhausted and in shock at the proposal. But the thought of going to America and of Angel being free was powerful.

Father Tom stood up and said, 'It is dinner time. Say no more until after dinner and take your time to think over what has been said. I have all the necessary paperwork with me. If we all agree, I'll have everything in order. I just have to get the paperwork to America and see that it is all official. Names, places and everything. Come on down for dinner and we'll talk about the weather to give you a break. I know by the looks on your faces that you are stunned.'

'So am I,' said Mary.

'And me too,' Michael added. 'Although we talked this over with Tom, when it comes down to putting it to you, it feels a whole lot different. But the thing is that it all rests with you, Frank and Molly, and Angel's entire future depends on what decisions you make. It's not easy, but it is your choice, she is your child. Angel will always be your child – she is old enough and wise enough to know who she is no matter where she is or what she is called.'

'Michael Junior and his wife will look after her just like their own,' Mary added. 'We've written to them all about her. We'll read out the letters to you if you want. They're looking forward to seeing her. They love her already! We all think you would be giving Angel a real chance at life by letting her do this. And you will be brought over too. We are arranging that as well. You mustn't be seen getting on the boat together – the three of you, or even the four of us together. They are getting very wise to how things are done so it will have to be very well planned. We can't all just get on a boat together and land in America.'

✳ *Chapter 18* ✳

*T*hey gave him a big clap at the table, but I wasn't listening anymore. I was thinking about Angel so I missed loads of what he was saying. Frank didn't hear it either I think. But when I eventually paid attention to what he was saying again, we were all finished dinner.

'I'll have to be getting back or they'll think I ran away and got married.' Father Tom was joking with everyone, and there were loud shouts of laughter all round the table. We had never heard a priest talking so openly. Where we came from, you would have to be someone important before a priest would speak to you, but Father Tom talked to everyone and anyone no matter who they were.

He stood up. 'Now Molly, you and Mary go off round the gardens for a bit of a stroll and a chat, and we'll have a talk with Frank here.'

The men went off into another room they called a 'smoking room', and me and Mary and another woman whose name I didn't even know went off for a walk. There were lovely gardens with trees and flowers and what have you, but my mind was troubled all the time and I couldn't enjoy these beautiful things.

'Mary,' I said. 'I don't know what to think. I feel devastated. I don't know what to say or what to do and I think Frank is in the same position. I tell you it's making me ill thinking of it.'

'Well,' said Mary smiling, 'I wouldn't make a bad granny.'

'Indeed you wouldn't, Mary,' I answered. 'I couldn't wish for a better granny for Angel. I don't know where to start and I don't know whether I'd be saying the right things or not. I'm just so exhausted now Mary, that nothing really matters to me any more, only Angel and her welfare. I can see she has adapted to working and all in the hotel. I think we've brought enough damage to her life and if changing her name is going to cause more, I don't think I'd be able to go through with it.'

'I know that,' says Mary. 'There's no doubt about that.'

'When it all boils down,' I went on, 'it will have to be Angel's own decision.'

When I said those words, I felt different. I don't know

how to put it, as if I knew the decision Angel would make and that I would be satisfied.

'Of course,' said Mary, 'I don't doubt that but Angel will want to know how you feel about it.'

I think my mind was decided somehow for I said, 'I don't think that's the way at all, Mary. It is Angel's decision. She's been through the mill already and this will put her through it again. Me and Frank will talk tonight and come to a decision. It has cost you a lot to stay the length of time you stayed here and for our tickets and all the other money spent on us – a small fortune it's costing you.'

'Money is for spending, Michael always says,' laughed Mary, 'and we have a bit to spend. This is something we want to do. For you and Frank and Angel, sure, but for other people around Ireland too. We will be going back very shortly and I hope to have you and Angel with us. But as you say Molly, that's Angel's decision. And Frank's. I just want to know how you feel.'

'Well, the way I feel,' I told Mary, 'is that I'd be agreeable. I don't say I'd be agreeable to go to America but I would be agreeable to let Angel go because I don't want to stand in her way of any possibility for happiness and a career. We have no destiny but she has. It's not for me to say at the moment but that's the way I feel.'

It started to rain so we rambled back to the house and we went in past the smoking room. There was great talk and noise going on there – people speaking and clapping. So we carried on to the other room and a maid came out to serve us tea. My mind was on the way Frank used to come in at home and we'd go to the room and he'd tell me about the boys and I'd tell him what was happening with me and the girls. All of a sudden there was a loud clap and the door opened and out came the men, including some strangers I hadn't seen before. They all had glasses in their hands. Father Tom came up to me.

'He's a very intelligent man, your husband, and he knows his stuff. He'll fill you in on everything. We had a great meeting now, but your case didn't come up. There were other matters we were discussing. How the country is being managed and what they all are trying to get done. You and Frank can make your decision this evening sometime.' Then he asked the maid to show us up to our room.

It was a lovely bedroom with chairs and everything, and a fire lit. We sat and looked at one another for about five minutes, without a word.

Then Frank said, 'I don't know what to do, Molly.'

I answered him, 'I don't either.'

'Well, that's a good start.' He smiled a bit. 'I was trying to think, but I couldn't with the meeting that was going on down there. I'll tell you what we'll do. My decision,' he said, 'is to do what Father Tom says.'

'I think the same, Frank.'

'But,' he went on, 'it's really up to Angel.'

'I said the same thing, Frank. That it is up to Angel.'

'I wonder how she will take it,' says Frank. 'What do you think of America?'

'Frank.' I looked straight into his eyes saying this. 'It would be great to get to America. All we're losing is our name and her name. Sure her first name can be changed any time but it is her surname that can't be interfered with. Do you know?'

'And what do you think of the christening?' asked Frank.

'What she deserves. As Father Tom says, she was neither christened nor confirmed nor nothing so far as the records go. She wasn't treated like a human being at all so if I can see her christened again it would do my heart good.'

'The same with me,' he agreed. 'I know she's a bit big for christening but even so, it would be recorded properly this time. So we'll say no more until Angel is here and see what she says.'

We lay back in the bed and fell asleep. We must have been about two hours in dreamland when I woke up all of a sudden. 'Frank, wake up!' I shook him.

Frank jumped up and says, 'Oh my God, what will they think? We sleeping and they all below in the sitting room'

It was getting on for five o'clock in the evening and Mary and Michael and Father Tom started laughing when we arrived downstairs.

'You are awful people for sleep in this country. No doubt

about it. There is no time for sleeping in America!' and he was joking and teasing us for a while. Then he asked, 'Did you talk?'

We told him our thoughts and how we would have to discuss it with Angel and see what she wanted to do.

'Well, the good news is,' said Father Tom, 'that first thing in the morning Angel will be here. I know myself it's up to Angel but it's up to you too. Angel is the main character in this drama, and it's her decision. She will have to have a day or so to think it over. We appreciate that. It is an awful thing to have to say to your own daughter but there is no other way. We'll get up early in the morning and see what happens. And we'll have a few drinks too,' he says. 'We're not about to go to bed if there's a few drinks to be had!'

And there was a big laugh and a clap from some of the men who were there. They were all great men at the whiskey, anyway, whatever about anything else.

We had a big spread for tea that evening and some of the men started singing traditional Irish songs. There was a man there with a fiddle and the woman of the house played the piano.

Tomorrow we had to face Angel and this big decision. This was the sad end of the matter. This was either the making or the breaking of us. We had the few drinks with everyone else and had good conversation and so the evening ran late into the night.

Father Tom gave us all a blessing. Mary and Michael came over and she said, 'We have a big surprise for both of you tomorrow.'

'Not another one,' laughed Frank.

'No. This will bring tears to your eyes. You're going to see what a bit of kindness and a bit of confidence in people can do. So goodnight, and we'll see you in the morning.'

We went on upstairs to bed. We felt very happy in one another's arms because with all the trouble and hassle we'd had, that bit of our life was slipping away as well.

We woke at seven o'clock next morning because we heard people and horses going round the yard outside. To our surprise, there were about twenty more people there who were not there the day before. The place was practically full. The minute we appeared, everyone gave us a big clap. They already knew our story and wanted to see Angel as well – the girl who had posed as a boy for years and carried it off and never made a mistake. 'The best girl ever reared, someone said. Somebody else shouted that a car was coming up the road. It was a drizzly morning outside.

'Now,' said Father Tom, 'you all know what to do when she gets out of the car.'

I saw it was Joe Sweeney's car when it came near the house. Joe hopped out and opened the other door. Angel came out all dressed up in a lovely dress and new shoes and with a new hair-do. She was amazed at all the people looking at her and, the minute she stepped out, everyone started cheering and clapping. They gave her a reception like she was royalty! She was so excited. She came running over to me and Frank then, and put her arms around us that tight I nearly couldn't breathe. I knew that she missed us terribly. This was going to be our day. This was a good day for her and a very bad day for us but she didn't know anything about that yet.

She was put at the head of the table for breakfast. Four or five women served us all at this big long table. I'll never forget it. It was like a hotel. I could barely eat the breakfast. Frank would nudge me and say, 'Eat up, eat up', and I'd say, 'You eat Frank', and Angel would give us a quick look down the table. She must have seen something in our faces and thought we were arguing or fighting or something, but we weren't. We were just not able to eat because we had this lump in our stomachs thinking of what we had to tell her and why she was here. After breakfast was over, Angel went round to each person to introduce herself. Michael came over to us and said, 'I know it is early in the morning but about this surprise we have for you ...'

'What is it, Mary?' I called over to her.

Mary turned to Angel and said, 'Angel go over to the piano and play for your Mam and Dad and the rest of us.'

Didn't Angel walk up to the piano just the same as if she were a film star and start playing? She played a song called 'The Spinning Wheel' and she sang it too. I had never heard

Angel singing like this before. Can you imagine that? Me, her mother! Her name was Angel and she was singing like an angel. I thought it was the loveliest singing I ever heard. The tears were running out of Frank's eyes and mine. The next thing she played was an Irish lament. She played a few more tunes and everybody clapped her as she took a little bow. Oh, she was a real little madam!

'So what do you think of that, Mam and Dad?' she asked.

'I can't believe it!' me and Frank both said together.

'Joe's wife taught me how to play. I love it,' she told us.

Father Tom came over and, after a bit of talk and listening to everyone praising Angel, said, 'I think Molly, Frank and Angel, you'd better go and discuss your bit of business. I've got word I can only stay another two days. I have to get back.'

So we went up to our room. The maid had lit the fire there for us and had put out lemonade for Angel and a drink for Frank and myself. We started by asking her how she felt about her job and the bit of education she was getting in the hotel.

'I never was as happy in all my life,' she told us excitedly. 'It is a godsend we met those people.'

'What do you think of Mary and Michael?' I asked.

'I love them,' she answered unhesitatingly.

'Would you have any problem,' I said, 'going back to America with them?'

She opened wide her big blue eyes and looked at us.

'Why?'

'I'm just asking,' I said. 'You don't want to go back to the life we had on the road or back to Meath, do you?'

'No way! No, I don't. I never want to hide again. Not for as long as I live. I feel so happy and free now. Going to America is my biggest dream!'

'Well,' I said, 'your Dad will explain to you what has to be done and we want you to listen. We don't want an answer on the spot. But we do in a few hours. Father Tom is going back and he's our only hope – Father Tom and Michael and Mary. You know we can't stay too long at the farm either. We have to move on because although the farmer got us a six-month extension, that could change overnight.'

'Come on,' she said, a bit anxiously. 'Tell me what you're suggesting.'

'You can't go to America without papers. You're not christened as far as Father Tom is concerned. You are not on a register. You couldn't go to school or anything in America unless you had these documents.'

'What would I have to do?'

'Well, first you'd have to change your name and get a new identity, have another surname. Father Tom says he would baptise you.'

'What name?' she asked.

'Michael and Mary's son wants you to be named after

Mary and his wife Jane as if you were Michael Junior's child from birth.'

'I would have to lose my mother and father and lose my name to go to America?' she exclaimed. 'Is that what you are saying?'

We talked about it all a bit more and we told her she would never lose us and we would never lose her. Then we told her to stay there in the room for a while to think about it all. We said to take about an hour.

Me and Frank went out the door and walked down the long corridor to the stairs. We stood there amazed at ourselves and at what seemed to be happening to us all. And we cried like two babies. We didn't know what we had done. But we had told Angel the story. That was hard. If she refused to go, at least she'd always remember we made an effort to do this for her.

When we went into the room below, Father Tom wanted to know how she'd reacted. 'She's in a kind of a daze above on her own,' I told him.

'Maybe I ought to go up,' he suggested.

'No,' I told him, 'she wants Mary and Michael to go up in about an hour. So I think it would be as well to give her the bit of time on her own.'

We all sat around pretending to be talking about this and that but we kept looking up at the stairs. We felt sad, myself and Frank, but what could we do? After about an hour, Michael and Mary went up the stairs. They were about fifteen minutes gone, when we heard their footsteps coming back down. Angel was with them, her arms around the two of them. It was a lovely sight to see, but it made me so very, very sad.

'I've made up my mind, Dad and Mam. I'm going with Mary and Michael. I'll do as they say because it might help you for me to go. But I love you. I'll agree with whatever Father Tom says and from now on I'll do as I'm told.'

There was a clap from the few people there and we hugged her and kissed her and Father Tom said to her, 'I have something else for you, Angel. Come on down here, down to the small room. I have something nice to show you. And everybody, come too.'

So off we all trooped to Father Tom's room. He opened the door and let us all in. There was a little homemade altar and a small water font there. 'For your christening, Angel, for your christening. And there on the table are all your papers. Your name, your register, everything you'll ever need is in this folder here. I am happy to be your parish priest when you come over to America. I am delighted for you, and for Molly and Frank. If you look around Angel, you will see some of the people who have helped. They are here today to see you christened and to witness something important happening in Ireland. Not alone will you have a new name, but you will now have a great future.'

Angel just said, 'I can't believe it but I'm ready.'

Father Tom put a white vestment around her and brought her over to the water font. Mary and Michael were the godparents and we stood around holding candles as he christened her with the water saying, 'In the name of the Father and of the Son and of the Holy Ghost, I baptise you Mary Jane O'Connell from America …' We all watched the water flow over her lovely hair as she bent her head down over the font.

Afterwards, we had music and singing and dancing. Angel sang and played the piano again. And she danced. She danced around and around the floor – even on her own, and it beat all!

❄ *Chapter 19* ❄

*E*veryone looked solemn, even tearful, at us going. They stood at the door waving and you know, it was a real good feeling. It was lonely but it was a good feeling. We'd had a good few days with them and we had made a hard decision – they understood, for they all had families too.

Anyway, we got to Sweeney's hotel. All the young girls that worked there gathered around Angel, talking excitedly. She was dying to tell them what happened and went off with them giggling and laughing. They talked all night and she was happy.

But the sad day had to come – and come it did the following Sunday.

Joe Sweeney had organised a bit of a session on the Saturday night after closing time. The farmer and his wife stayed overnight as well to say their goodbyes to Angel.

Joe said, 'Soon we'll see what the next step for you is going to be but we won't discuss you for the minute. It is great to see her getting this chance. That girl has a head on her shoulders. She's on the way and when she settles down in America, she'll have it made because they will all just love her. And it won't be long before I'll be over there, me and the wife and children, to join her as well. Till then any letters will come to me here and I'll read them out to you. And I'll write back for you as long as I'm here because no one else can see those letters. They have to be destroyed once they're read. We don't want to get into trouble.'

Frank said we had a lot to think over.

So we had Angel settled now. She was looking forward to going and she was happy, we knew that, but we were going to miss her.

Joe saw how we felt and said, 'Look Molly, if she was with you all these months and then just went off to America you'd have felt a lot worse. Now at least you see what she can do when she has her independence. She can play the piano, she can sing, she can do things. She is going to be a bright student and the family she's going to will give her their full attention. She's very lucky, if you could call it that. I know 'twill be heartbreaking to see her sailing off – and that you can't even go down to the port with her. That's bad but it's the way the men want to handle her departure to minimise any risks of trouble. You know that yourselves.'

'We know,' Frank nodded. 'Joe, we understand it well.'

When the bar closed, the customers went home and we started up the little party. Everyone was very good to us. They would look at us and we knew what they were thinking.

Frank said to me, 'You can see it in everyone's eyes that we are a pity, but we have another decision to make here tonight and we'll have to tell Angel straight in front of Mary and Michael and Joe and his wife and all the friends. I have something else I want her to agree to.'

'And what's that, Frank?'

'Well, you know what,' he said, 'you can tell me to shut up later on if you don't like what I have to say.' And we left it at that.

The night went on and Joe hit a glass with a spoon for everyone's attention. 'Frank wants to say something,' he announced. Everyone starting clapping and calling, Speech, speech!

'I've no speech for ye,' Frank said, standing up so he could see everyone. 'There is something I want to say to Angel and the people here that helped us out through all our troubles. I am delighted that Angel is getting her chance in life. I know she is going to do very well. But I am going to ask her something in front of everyone here tonight. I want to ask are you happy, Angel?'

'I am, Dad,' she answered.

I wanted to ask Frank what this was all about but I couldn't. He continued talking to Angel: 'Well, Angel. I want to say something to you and Molly.' And he stopped for a long time and everybody was looking at him and at me and the quiet was terrible.

'Molly, I am not leaving my three lads behind. I'm not going to America. But if you want to go, Molly, I'll take my chance on my own.'

'Well, Frank Maguire, aren't you the right eejit!' I shouted back at him in surprise. And everybody burst out laughing. Angel half laughed, half cried, too. But I went on in a loud voice, 'I was thinking the very same thing. You said it before me. I don't want to leave my three boys alone in the graveyard.'

'So what do you think, Angel?' says Frank.

'I know you don't want to leave my brothers. I even said it to Mary and Michael. I knew you wouldn't desert them. You didn't abandon me and you are not going to abandon them. I love you very much and my heart is breaking when I think of you leaving the boys behind. It would be different if they had relations to visit them and put flowers on their graves. But I'm going to go to America and I'm going to make good what was done to us. It might take me a lifetime but I am going to make sure this happens to nobody else. The same as Michael and Mary. I am going to study and do my best for people who are harassed by the law. I love you but I knew you would want to stay.'

There was a big clap from everyone. Angel came running over to us and, of course, the tears were flying out of all our eyes. The people left us alone then and they all talked among themselves. And Angel and Frank and me talked together.

'I couldn't leave the boys,' Frank said. 'I want to be buried beside them.'

'So do I, Frank,' I said to him. 'They need us too. At least Angel will have someone to love her and help her but the boys have nobody. I know they are in Heaven. They couldn't be anywhere else.'

Then Frank said, 'After Angel goes, we'll find our way back to Meath where the children are buried. That's where I want to die. I couldn't go away to America.'

He put his arms around me and he says, 'I knew you wouldn't go, Molly. You're an old softie like myself.'

'I'm glad,' says Angel, 'that you decided this together.'

'Why I announced this tonight,' said Frank, 'was just in case anyone would think I was persuading Molly about not going. I wanted to say it out of the blue and say this is the way I am feeling. I think Molly understands what I mean.'

'I do, Frank,' I said. 'I know you too well. We started off together and we are going to finish together. So long as I know you're well Angel, and looked after, that is good enough for me. At least we saved one.'

'That's right, Molly,' says Frank, 'one out of four.'

'We can't turn back the clock now, Frank. We have to put the clock on instead of back. There is no going back for Angel. She is the little bit of hope we have. We'll never forget you Angel, and we know you'll never forget us even though we might never see you again once you're in America.'

'How could I forget the best parents in the world?' Angel said, giving us both a huge hug. 'You are the best parents any child could have.'

They were great words to come out of Angel's mouth and she so young. She had it all behind her now but she was very wise.

After the little party we went off up to bed. I woke in the middle of the night and I could hear Frank sobbing in his sleep. I had the sheet in my mouth trying to stop myself from crying.

We came down the next morning. All the suitcases were in the lobby and we looked at one another. Oh God, this is it, we knew. All Angel's little bits and pieces were there. We could hear talking – Angel was in a room with her friends, saying her goodbyes. They looked happy enough.

So in comes Michael and Mary. 'The time has come,' said Mary. 'We have to go. It's awful that you can't come down to the quayside to see us off but we'll be praying for you and we'll write. We'll let you know how she's getting on and if she's unhappy we'll bring her back. It'll take her time to settle down with her new family.'

Joe Sweeney announced that it was time to go. 'We have a half an hour to get there and get fixed up. I want you to say your goodbyes now and don't come out until we're gone.'

Me and Frank just stood there, devastated, heartbroken and tearful. What else we did that morning, I can't remember. We didn't know whether to sit down or walk or run or what to do. Angel got in between us and we kissed the faces off of each other. We told her that we would always be there with her and told her lies – sure we knew we were losing our lovely child, that we'd never see her again. Until we were all in Heaven.

Joe was a tower of strength that morning. 'Come on now, we have to go. America is calling.' He was laughing and I knew by his face that he was trying to lighten things.

A man came in and started bringing out the cases to this kind of open truck he had. There was lots of luggage in it. It had to go separately down to the docks. Angel was weakening as she went out the door, and so were we, gone at the knees. That was as far as we could go – the door.

'Come on, Angel,' says Joe. 'Don't look back.'

And my lovely girl did just that. She looked at us both with her big watery eyes, turned, and with Mary's arms around her, walked out to the car. We could see her blonde hair as they drove off.

It was terrible. We cried. The two of us cried.

Frank caught my arm and said, 'Come on. Down the beach to watch the ship going out. We'd better hurry – it is a long way off and we have to go roundabout and not be seen.'

We went off about a mile out the road. We were in a half-trot. We got to the beach near a lighthouse. We knew exactly where to stand and watch for we had often been there watching the boats before. About three-quarters of an hour went by and next thing the front of the ship came out of the harbour. The horn blew a few times just then. There was no one else around and we stood for ages until the ship went out of sight. It started getting dark and cold. We were two very lonely people.

It took us a long time to get back to the hotel, sick from crying and our hearts broke. I just said, 'God take us now, take us on this spot. Don't make us suffer any more than this.'

Joe and Joan and a couple of others made us as comfortable as they could back at the hotel. Joe knew how much pain we were in, but he was always on the up-and-up.

'You'll have to try and pull yourselves together,' he said. 'You've been through a lot but don't let Angel down. Come on and face the storm as it is. I know it's easy for me to say but I know what you are going through. She has gone off with good people and she's going to do very well for herself. I'll come out with any letters. I'll read them to you while I can. But things are tightening up here and we're being watched. They know there's something afoot. They just don't know what. But here is some news for you. Angel's friends here – they're all off to America very soon. They are, every one of them, daughters of people run out of the country. Some of them might be able to join their people but a lot of them never will. The like of Mary and Michael and Michael Junior know the score. I'll be putting the hotel up for sale in a few months when I've done as much as I can. It won't be safe for me anymore. I have a few buyers interested. I wouldn't last in this country. My feelings are too strong. We'll be able to do a lot more from America and other people will take over here. We have to keep changing because they get to know us. So for God's sake, don't give up on yourselves now. It's tough. It's hard. But that's the way it is.'

Frank just said, 'All right.' He had a few whiskeys and I had a few sherries. It took nothing to make us cry. Just looking at each other was enough for us to start.

We never slept a wink that night. We could hear the ships in the harbour blowing their horns and that made it worse. We knew our little girl was gone over the seas for America without us. We just couldn't leave our three dead boys. We wanted to be buried with them. And we were glad that we could give Angel the chance. You'd know by her face going out the door that she knew it was the end. That we would never be together again. That was the pain.

We went out to the farm and cried like babies all over

again. We couldn't have a conversation because Angel came into it every time.

Up in the cottage, Frank said to me, 'You know Molly, I have to go out and do some work tomorrow.'

'We have to keep busy. Angel is with good people.'

Frank worked all day and came to the house for dinner. This went on for days, and we were afraid to meet one another face to face during the day because we'd start crying or mention something or come across something in the cottage belonging to Angel. That used to kill us. It changed our whole lives. Everything was over and we knew ourselves our lives were over too. There was only the waiting. We had done our best. We thought we had done the best thing, anyway.

Angel knew there was nothing left for her in Ireland but the open road. She had no other choice but to take the opportunity Father Tom and Mary and Michael gave her. And she knew us better than we did ourselves. There was one question on our minds though – when were we going to hear from her?

A couple of weeks went by before Joe Sweeney arrived with the first letter. He read it out to us. I can remember it word for word:

Dear Mam and Dad,

Arrived in America and it is a lovely place. I would love to have you here with me. I've new friends now and I am starting school next week. Everything is great. Thanks for all you've done for me. I am very lonesome for you and I hope to God some day things will work out for you. No one could ask for a better Mam and Dad than I've had, and I still have you. I know you had a big decision to make and so had I, but I wish you all the best of luck and may God look after you.

Father Tom says he'd say a prayer at his Masses every morning for you. For you and Dad, to help you to cope with the problems of your lives and that God will be good to you and look after you and that's all for now, Mam and Dad. I'll write again when I get time.

All my love.
Your daughter Angel.

'Well, what do you think of that?' I said to Frank.

'She's settling in,' he said.

'That's something to be happy for,' I said.

There was nothing in the letter to hurt us or suggest she wanted to come home.

'I had a letter from Mary and Michael and the son,' said Joe Sweeney. 'She's helping out in the new house and getting on fine with them. She has her new identity and passport all sorted and handed in the day they arrived. She just slipped through and now she's right for life.'

More time went by, and our six months with the farmer was almost up. We had a few more weeks before the law might be out shifting us on. We got a few more letters. Angel was settled down, everything was great; she started school and she had great friends. She was still doing her piano and thinking of us every day.

Joe Sweeney read them all to us. One day he said, 'The letters will be getting shorter now.' He didn't say what he meant. Then he told us he got an offer on the hotel.

'Well, our time is up too,' I told him. 'We'll have to be making tracks soon.'

Joe came out another day and he had another letter. Angel said that she'd heard he was coming out and might start a hotel business there.

'I've sold the hotel and we're off in three weeks,' he said next time he was out. 'I'm having an auction and we'll sell everything. They know I hold meetings in the hotel, Frank. Word gets round very quick. You don't know who you're talking to in this country these days and you don't know who is coming in and out. So long as they have a job themselves they don't care about anyone else. Anyway, there is no time for another letter but I'll write something out for you. I'll come out next week and I'll write a good letter for you to Angel and you'll have to say goodbye in the letter because no more letters can come. You're going to have no address for letters to get to you. The farmer is being watched as well and the post could be opened. We don't know at the minute but you could count that as your last letter. I'll bring one with me to America for you.'

We said thanks for all he did for us and Angel, and for the hospitality he and Joan gave us.

'That's nothing,' he says. 'We have a victory. That's the way to take it. But I can do no more here because my time has come to go. It wouldn't be too long more before the authorities find out who I am and what I do. I don't stand for the things they want. This is why I get no work at the courts – I defend the poor people. When I get to America we can do what we like. But it'd be as well for you and Frank to say your goodbyes in your letter. If they ever found out where she is and who she's with they'd track us all.'

But sure we knew well what the story was even if we never knew the details.

'It's all right,' says Frank. 'We know she is happy enough and getting educated. I suppose a father and mother can't ask for any more. Maybe some day she'll come back and see us either in our graves or alive – you never know. Stranger things happened to us already.'

A few days later I was talking to the farmer about the Sweeneys going.

'Isn't it sad,' he said. 'We lose our friends by the day. They have to earn a living but they just can't find a living in their own country. But there is always someone to take their place. That is one thing that we have: for the one that leaves we have two to take their place. We are going from strength to strength and it's the likes of Joe Sweeney and Michael and Mary and their son and all the rest that can get things moving. It'll be a great country some day. So maybe your time is coming. It is breaking my heart to see the two of you going, but things are tightening up.'

Back at the cottage, Frank said, 'It's final, Molly. We have to let everything go. We'll just say good things in the letter for whoever will be reading it.'

'The two of us left as we started out,' I said. 'The two of us together. We have that.'

'We'll just carry on,' said Frank. 'We just have to figure out how we are going to get back on the road and where we are going to go.'

'I know where I am going, Frank,' I said. 'Back to where our trouble started. I want to be beside the boys.'

'And so do I, Molly,' he says. 'I was just testing the water with you there to see did you want to chance somewhere else. Didn't Angel say she saw the boys in her dreams?'

'That's right Frank, I forgot about that.'

'That's keeping me going, her and the boys. And you know,' he added with a bit of a laugh, 'things are not as bad as they look.'

Joe Sweeney arrived out one evening. 'I had a great auction; I made a good few pounds. Everything's sold. I'm packed and ready for moving. We're to stay with a friend for a week and then we're away.'

He went back out to the car and came in with two heavy bags. 'Money!' he says. 'All the change from the hotel that I saved over the years, pennies and shillings and sixpences and thruppences. It's for you. You can't go round and flash pound notes, but this'll keep you going for a while until something turns up.'

He ignored all our protestations. 'What am I going to do with it anyway? I can't bring it to America.' He was laughing. 'I'd look well going over with an Irish penny!'

He told us he would be out during the week and would write the letter. Me and Frank went up to the cottage again with the two bags of money. We had about a score apiece!

'We have travelling money,' says Frank, and he laughed.

'That's right,' I agreed. 'It's Travellers' money not travelling money you have.' And we had a giggle.

'It is good to see you laughing again, Molly, it does my heart good.'

'Maybe the whole thing didn't happen. Maybe we'll wake up tomorrow morning, back the way we were and realise that all these disasters never happened.'

I sighed and gave him a smile. But it did happen and we had to put up with it.

'And we know it happened, Pat. It's not a dream. It's reality. It's our situation now that I am thinking about. We're back under the canvas again and the cold and the damp. We won't be able for that much longer, myself and Frank. We've had years and years of it. Too many. It was great when we were out of it, having proper food and things like that. We miss that for sure at our age. This kind of life, we're not able for it now.'

'I know Molly, I know,' Frank said to her, 'but we have to manage. We have to manage the same as every other person. We were just lucky to meet people who helped us. We have to be thankful for that.'

'I know that, Frank. But you know yourself we are not going to live too long …'

'Ach, I don't know 'bout that, Molly. We're hardy old devils!' Frank gave a bit of a laugh.

'But the good was taken out of us from working day and night and living in wet places. That's all going to come against us. My knees are sore, my feet are sore, my back is sore …'

'And so are mine,' cut in Frank. 'That's what they call getting old!'

They were ignoring me now, working this out between themselves. I could tell they had had this conversation before.

'Exactly. So long as we accept that. We don't want any miracles. Only that we won't be caught, Frank. They're still after us – they'll never leave us alone. But we'll never be caught. We'll live as long as we can. We can watch them and every time they pass us by, we can think of what they done to us. But what can we say? If we open our mouths, we're destroyed. As you said yourself, better to die unknown than to die in jail. We've done what we had to do and we got our story across to young Pat here. Some day it might do some good for someone – at least someone will know what happened to us.

'We'll just take each day as it comes and do what we can to keep one another alive. I hope we have a few years left so we can look at these people and see them face to face. They won't recognise us after all these years; they won't know who we were maybe. A generation on the road we are.'

'In life, Pat, everyone is hurt some way,' Molly said to me. 'Look at our story – it was so bitter and ended up so bad. Maybe the only one who won out of it was Angel. But she lost her mother and father and we lost her and our three sons. So it isn't a nice story to be trying to tell anybody. Especially when some of the people are still alive. But, like everything else, somebody had a bit of luck out of it in the end.

'Only for the police and the people in the big estates – they don't want to see Travelling people settling in anyway – we could've been all right and have Angel still with us. But it wasn't to be. Anyway, I had better go back and finish the story for you, Pat.'

The week after the Sweeneys left, the farmer called Frank in.

'I believe you're getting ready, Frank.' he said.

'I am,' Frank told him. 'I don't know what way I'll manage.'

'Come up to the yard. I want to show you something. I had a carpenter friend of mine up when you were away and he did a bit of a job.'

'Ha! I seen the shed locked,' remarked Frank. 'Were you afraid the carts would come out without the horse?'

'No, no!' the farmer started laughing. 'I have something in here for you.' He took the lock off the door and opened it and there was the wagon that we came down in.

'I am giving you back your wagon and I got a young horse off a friend of mine,' he explained. 'It's up there in the far field. You can have the horse. So you can go back the same way as you came. And I have letters for you to deliver for me, Frank, important letters. I want you to go back over the same road that you came down and go into the same farmers as well. Will you do that for me?'

'I will,' said Frank. 'No better man.'

'And be careful,' the farmer told him, 'because if you're caught with these letters it will mean very big trouble, I'm telling you. These are very important. I want you to give them to these people and just show them the names on the envelopes. Just show them and each one will take their own.'

'That's no problem,' Frank promised. 'I'll deliver the letters.'

'You're good people, and these people will look after you till you get to Meath. But after that, Frank, you are on your own. You know what you are facing up there.'

'I know,' Frank answered. 'I am facing a graveyard full of children belonging to me and Molly. That is what I am going up to face and that's where I am ending, up there. But I can't thank you enough for what you done for us. You made life worth living; you showed us kindness and took us in as strangers off the roads. I don't know if I would do the like myself to be honest.'

'We just do our best, for you and for the Cause,' said the farmer.

Frank nodded. 'When do you think we should shift?' he asked.

'Two days more and the six months are up and mark my words, they'll be out here. I have a fella coming down to take over the cottage and he can stay for a while but I don't think they'll give him six months. We were lucky.'

'Two days is grand,' Frank said.

We were very lonely in the cottage that night because we knew we were going. The farmer couldn't afford to keep us any longer with the police watching. We got up at six o'clock the morning we were going. The farmer had the horse and the whole lot ready. Food packed in the wagon, everything. He had no money to give us, but he gave us plenty of food, and the letters, to help us along the way as well. Back to square one – the farmer sad, his wife crying, me crying and Frank looking miserable and us locked in each other's arms. It was one of the saddest things I ever went through. It was sad with Angel going and it was sad again leaving the farmer and his wife because we knew well we wouldn't see them again or even hear of them or any of the people who had helped us because we couldn't read or write or anything like that. We had to listen to people to find out what was going on, and then you would never hear too much, you know. So we said our goodbyes and got into the wagon and were away down the lane for the Dublin road out of Cork.

We travelled all that day and we pulled in on the side of the road. The next morning we headed for the nearest place to get the horse a drink. We went on and came to the first farm we were to stop at, the last place we were at on the way down. They welcomed us and pulled our cart into the yard and put it away out of sight. They brought us in and let us wash ourselves. Frank took out the letters and your man picked his letter out of the bundle. 'That one's for the next fella. He's about ten miles up the road and he might keep ye for a while. He has the work. You can bed down here for the night and be off in the morning.'

So we did that and it wasn't too bad. You see, the wagon was well made. Well insulated and there were no draughts or even cold in it. We had plenty of blankets. We had a good sleep and a good breakfast. The farmer gave us a bag of food

wrapped in a pillow slip and we put it into the cart, shook
hands with him again and went on.

We went the ten miles that day and pulled into this other
farm. We spent two days there as the farmer's man was gone
on the run and he wanted a hand. We did the work and he
gave us a few pound as well.

We went twenty miles the next day to another farm. We
stayed the night in the yard for he had no room in the house.
We went off the next day. We were travelling for days and
days. We met Travellers on the way and pulled into their
camps at night. There was an awful lot of people on the move
those days – they wouldn't be allowed to stay any more than
a night or two and they had to move on. We were safe when
we travelled with them.

We had delivered our last letter to a man who made no
comment, just gave us a bit of food and told us we had to
keep moving because he said the authorities were on to him
and he couldn't be seen helping us out. 'If you're stopped,' he
says, 'going down the road, say you went up looking for sugar
or tea or something and you got none. We're not supposed
to give you anything you know, you'd count as begging and
that's an offence.'

Then one day, years later, after all our wanderings and un-
certainties, we found ourselves in Kildare, near Dublin. Age
was getting at us I suppose and we wanted to go home. To

where we are now, I mean; this is the only home we have, beside the boys. We recognised the farm we had stopped at years before, but nobody there recognised us.

We came near Dublin the next day and pulled into a laneway where we cooked our meal. We lit a bit of a fire and the whole thing was terrible, it was all turning round for us again. Trying to light fires in the wet. You know, we'd look at each other as much as to say what did we put ourselves in for this time? So we went up to a farmyard outside the town on the Dublin road to ask about where could we sell the horse and cart so as we could get some money to buy a tent.

'Ah, you should have no bother if you go into Dublin where the markets are. People will buy that, horse and all.'

Eventually we went on to Dublin. There was a market on the day we got in and horses everywhere. It was very exciting because we were there before and it's nice to feel you know some place. This man came over.

'Are you selling that cart, the four-wheel wagon and the horse?'

'We are,' Frank said.

'I'll buy it off you but I won't give you much for it. What are you going to do without it?'

'We'll buy a tent,' Frank told him.

'Down the road there,' says he, 'go down and have a look – there is good tents there, army tents and the like. And you'd probably buy them cheap. Sure I'll go down with you. Tie the horse there.'

We tied the horse and went down. We picked out this tent here and got a second-hand bike and a big pram too. Your man paid for them. He took the horse and cart for it and he gave Frank a tenner.

'I can't take a note off you,' Frank told him.

'I know what you mean,' the man said. 'I'll get you the change.'

He went into a pub nearby. I'd noticed all the men walking in and out. There was no women allowed in a pub of course. He came out and gave us the money in shillings. So we shook hands with him and the deal was done. It was just the thing to do.

So we went off. Walking, wheeling the pram with the tent on the back-roads and side-roads. We camped in different places. If we saw Travellers, we'd pull in with them. One bunch of Travelling people were heading for Meath. They offered to bring the stuff for us if we wanted to go with them. There were four families altogether so we joined them. It took us a couple of days to get down and this here is where we came. The pram is out there and the old bike. Here we are and I don't think we can stay long either.

Molly had nearly come to the end of her story.

'We'll have to move,' she said to me, 'but I am very happy that

we met you, Pat. You're a good man or a good boy or whatever you like to call yourself. That was a great thing to do for us, to listen to our story.'

I looked at the two of them. 'Molly and Frank,' I said, 'that is the saddest story I ever heard in all my life. An atrocity it is. A scandal that you still have to hide.'

'We are still hiding Pat, and we will be to the day we are buried. We'll have to die unknown to everyone. No one will know who we were. The good people we left behind us know who we are. Trouble is, we don't know who we are ourselves anymore. We are back to square one again without any identity. But it doesn't matter now that we've told you our story. Don't tell it to anyone for a few years, Pat, not until the whole country changes and them people from the big estates is dead. The police won't care anymore then and you'll be safe. I hope it won't be a burden to carry but I wouldn't be telling anyone just yet. You'd only be getting yourself into trouble, Pat. You mightn't think it but we know so we do.'

❆ Chapter 20 ❆

'There is just a few odds and ends we have to try and remember,' Molly said to me then, 'just so that you'll understand why we're here.'

'Oh, but I do,' I told Molly. 'I understand why you're here. I have the gist of it now. I can see why you have to be so careful. It's just to know where you are going from here that's really bothering me now.'

'You're a young man,' she said. 'There's very little you could do for us. We're just afraid that they'll find out who we are around here and that'd finish us off. We'd sooner die in the open, than locked away inside somewhere. We won't be telling anyone about Angel. You're the only person we've told. I know it is all a good *while ago and the police have changed here now. They call 'em guards but the same type of people are in it. They used to call them peelers one time. They just changed their name. They still look out for the big man and the landlord.'*

'So, you're still not out of the woods?' I asked her.

'It is still the same. Some day they might recognise us – we can't last much longer here. There's a little nun, Sister Theresa, in the hospital there. She looks after me with a bit of clothes and food. She knows about us; she knows a bit of our story. But if they found out that she was doing anything for people like us, she'd probably be sent away somewhere else. Helping the likes of us, she has to be careful. I've to be careful going in. I just stand at the door just begging – which we have never done in our whole lives. But we have to live. She knows about you too, Pat. That we are telling you our story. She told me to be careful that no one sees you talking to us. That was what she said. So, Pat, you want to be very careful and not get yourself into any trouble. We're nearly at the end of our days and it doesn't matter, but you're like our Angel, only starting your life off.'

'I won't get myself into trouble, Molly,' I assured her. 'I can keep out of trouble. And if there is anything I can do for you I will.'

'Thanks – we don't know where we are going from here, if anywhere, but we are very grateful to you for listening, Pat. I won't trouble you much longer with our problems. You're a good listener but I'm sure you've better things to be doing.'

'It's been great having you here,' said Frank.

'Well,' I said, getting ready to go, 'it is a hard story but I enjoyed all the talk and you leave me a whole lot wiser than I was the first night I came. I'll keep your story alive. I can't right the wrong that was done to you. But if I can do anything else, just tell me.'

'Ah well,' she sighed, 'children grow up too and they have their views and their education and all. What about yourself?'

'Molly,' I said, 'there's not much education for me. I am out working. Just after my confirmation I had to go out to work and I didn't get educated at all. If I have children of my own, they'll be educated because I will make sure of it. And I'll tell them your story too.'

'Good man, Pat,' she says. 'And my last words to you now are God bless.'

The snow got worse and there was a storm rising. You could hear the wind whistling around the tent. I felt very sorry for them. Two lonely people. I was still young and had never seen anyone as unhappy; and still they were so friendly and they made a lot of you, as if you were important to them. And I didn't know then how important they were to me.

I said good night and shook hands and told them that if I was passing by again I'd drop in.

'You and Frank, you put a lot of stuff in my head and some day I'll tell your story and make people sit up and listen and thank God for what they have.' This was in my mind as I set off. It was *like a promise I made. 'Good night Molly, good night Frank!' I called back from outside in the snowflakes.*

'Good night,' called Frank, 'and thanks again, Pat, for listening to us.'

So I went off about my business. The night was getting bad. The snow came in a blizzard across the fields; the wind was whistling through the bushes and the trees were getting heavy with snow. I just got home in time that night, covered in snow. My mother was there and said, 'Will you have a cup of tea? I'm having one myself. Your Dad is in bed. Where on earth were you till now?'

'Down the town,' I lied.

It snowed heavily all night and the next day. It never stopped. The whole countryside was white and beautiful but I kept thinking of Molly and Frank below in the tent. I was at work the next two days and didn't pass by their place. The morning after that, I couldn't go anywhere. I heard the laneway was blocked, completely covered from ditch to ditch. I thought to myself they could never survive such nights in the bitter cold. But I was too young and thoughtless, or maybe too cowardly, to tell anyone about them. I can't forget that now.

It took three days for the snow to clear so that you could go down the laneway. I thought I'd head down and see could I get something hot for them. The thaw was on. I went off but I couldn't see anything. I got near the ditch where their campsite was. It was gone; everything was gone – the tent, the bike, the pram.

Oh my God, I thought to myself, they must have been able to get out of it. I wondered if they'd moved late that night but I knew they were too shaken up to go far after I'd gone home. I had found it hard enough.

As I was looking around the site, a man came along. I recognised him – he lived a couple of hundred yards up from where they had camped.

'Are you looking for something?' he called. He had an English accent.

'No,' I said, thinking quickly. 'The night of the snow I was coming up along here and lost my ring. Somewhere around where that camp was.'

'Those Travelling people were found dead yesterday. The two of them in each other's arms dead. The guards came up and took everything away. But they are looking for anyone who knew them. Did you know them?' he asked, looking me hard in the eye.

'No, I didn't. Did you?'

'How would I know them? I don't talk to Travellers. I thought I heard you talking to them a few nights ago. I was down in my garden and could hear voices.'

'Ha, that wasn't me anyway,' I laughed back at him. 'Sure I never even saw them.' I realised that he was trying to pump me for information.

'The guards said if I knew anyone that knew them, to tell them, and I am a man of the law,' he said. 'I don't know why people hide these people. They must be wanted for something because the guards are very interested in who they might be. I just thought it sounded like you.'

'Sure we all talk the same around here.' I knew he wouldn't contradict that for he had a different accent to everyone else.

'There was someone with them every night,' he said, 'nearly every night, anyway. I could hear talking when I went down the garden. Mind you, I kept awake at night too. I didn't want to be robbed.'

'They wouldn't do that,' I said. 'Not everyone like them is thieves.'

'They'd rob anything,' he said. 'I was going to get them shifted on anyway but by God now they're dead. They were brought to the hospital mortuary in town. The guards brought me in to see could I identify them. I couldn't. It was me who told them that they were there in the first place.'

He told me the guards said they must find out their names and who they were talking to. And why were they left there that long without anybody reporting them.

'Well, it's none of my business,' I said to him. I was upset by the news and angry at this selfish man who didn't care a bit about them.

'If you find a ring when the snow is all gone, would you let me know please?' I asked him. 'I only live up the road.'

'I know that well,' he said.

I realised that the first night was probably what had killed them and they'd been three days lying dead in the tent and it covered with snow. They probably just froze to death in their sleep.

When I got home my mother told me that the guards were round during the day enquiring about two people who died down the road in a tent in the snow and somebody who was visiting them. 'Isn't that shocking?' she said. 'If we knew they were there, we could have brought them in. You couldn't live out in that kind of night.'

So I told her about the man down the road who had reported them to the guards.

'Have people no compassion in them at all?' my mother exclaimed. 'That is just shocking. What else would you expect from him, anyway?'

'Why do you say that, Mam?' I asked, surprised at the sharp tone in her voice. 'That was the first time I ever talked to him but he knew me all right.'

'Well,' she told me, 'he used be in a Big House about four miles from here. And he was a bad one! His wife ran away on him. He was no good. The big estate had brought him over from England and he was worse than the people that owned the place. He wouldn't leave a stone unturned, no mercy for anyone.'

'Well,' I told her, 'the two people down there – it was me talking to them.'

'And why didn't you tell us about them?' my mother asked.

'I couldn't,' I told her. 'I promised them. They told me not to tell anybody. Their names were Molly and Frank Maguire and they used to work in that big estate.'

'Oh my God. Have mercy on their souls.' She sat down at the table in distress. 'Ah no, why ever didn't you tell me?'

'I promised them I'd tell nobody.'

'I knew the two of them well when I was growing up. They worked there and their three children died and they left in the middle of the night one night, with their little girl and disappeared.'

So I up and told my mother the whole story and she was upset at every word I said.

'Aye,' she said, 'it is a good thing that man down the road didn't recognise them. They must have got very shook looking with what happened to them. If he recognised them, he would have had them lifted on the spot because he was the head steward in the place at the time. But they'd be alive.

'You better mind yourself,' she warned me. 'If they find out it was you, they could say you were an accomplice. They made up awful things about them when they ran away – all sorts of ugly things. They would make you tell them the whole story. And you know, they might think it was just a poacher that stopped to talk to them too. You have to be very careful.' She was in a terrible state over it. 'I don't know what to do.'

'Do nothing,' I said. 'I want to see them in the mortuary but we can't go to the funeral. No one round here can go or they will only be accused of talking to them, you know.'

I went into work the next morning. The shop I worked in supplied the hospital. I was hoping that they had some messages for me to take so I could talk with Sister Theresa. It was a miracle or something, for the boss sent me over with a basket of groceries and milk.

I put the basket on the bike and sped over and into the kitchen where I often left the messages. One of the women in the kitchen pointed out Sister Theresa to me. I went up to her and said, 'I'm Pat – Molly and Frank's friend.'

'Oh,' she said, holding out her two hands to me, 'you're a very good boy,' making me feel embarrassed. 'Molly and Frank are laid out in the mortuary,' she told me. 'And there is a guard in and out keeping an eye on anyone coming to see them. They're looking for someone that was talking to them. They went through all their stuff and it would take a tear from a stone to see them go through their few belongings. They had nothing. They had no papers or anything to identify them either.'

'Can I see them?' I asked her.

'Ah, Pat,' she said, 'you can't. They're watching. They'd guess it was you or somebody belonging to you was talking to them. I was asked to take care of the funeral so they will be buried tomorrow. I know where to bury them,' she said. 'I went out this morning to see the grave-digger. So I got them right beside the children. You better keep away or we will all be in trouble.'

'It's bad that you can't go to a person's funeral.'

'There will be no one, only me and the priest and a man from the council. The guards will be there to see if anyone turns up. So, if I was you, I would just keep away and say a prayer for them. I know how you feel. Hunted down like criminals all their lives. You know the guards have a fair idea who they are but they want to see who was talking to them. I told them I never met them before, just that Molly came in for clothes, food and a few fags for Frank. I know their story and it is a sad one. So I would keep away. This is how it has to be. They will be brought out to the cemetery tomorrow and buried. I don't know what time it's at. Whenever the man with the coffins comes. But I will tell Frank and Molly that you will pray for them, and God forgive everyone that harmed them. I might see you when all this dies down, Pat, and we can have a talk about it. You come in all the time anyway.'

So I went home.

That is the end of the story. There should never be a return to the 'wormdiggers' castles' because every man, woman and child has the right to live in their own place nowadays. But that all came too late for Frank and Molly, and the boys. They lie in this abandoned graveyard. But they're happy to be back together.

And the wormdigger's daughter? Well, Angel was never seen nor heard from again. Nor was there ever any word of her visiting the graveyard. She could have, but if she did, nobody knows. I am not saying she didn't come back to see where her mother and father and three brothers are buried. Maybe she did, or maybe she wasn't able to return. Either way, I'm sure she never forgot her roots, and the sacrifices people made to keep her safe.

Author's Note

I want to thank everyone who helped me with this book. My own family, because without them I'd never have taken it on, even though I promised all those years ago to tell the story. I had a bit of it put down in writing, but then I was away for years. My family was reared and I got divorced. Then one of them found my notebook and the title made them curious; so they made me tell them the story. And then I put it all down for everyone else to read.

I want to thank in particular Caroline MacEvoy who put a great amount of time into transcribing all my tapes to get the manuscript together for me, and who helped to get the book on its way towards publication by introducing it to Seamus Cashman at BookConsulT. I appreciate her hard work and contribution very much and happily acknowledge her important role in enabling me to fulfil my promise to Molly and Frank.

I hope you enjoyed the story, tragic and all as it is, and that you will spare a thought for those poor people whenever you kneel down to pray.

About the author

John Farrell comes from near Navan in county Meath. The youngest of fourteen children, his people came from a labouring background and were involved in the Land League. His father worked for a time as an army chef. John was a messenger boy when he was a teenager. He later studied civil engineering in North London and worked in the construction industry for many years before returning to Ireland. He has three sons, two daughters and fourteen grandchildren.

The Sea's Revenge
& Other Stories
Séamus Ó Grianna

ISBN: 978 1 85635 413 4

Love, matchmaking, storytellers, emigration, feuding and fighting, Séamus Ó Grianna's subject matter revolves around the traditional life and lore of the Gaeltacht of his youth. His aim was never to be a modern, analytical, 'literary' writer but rather, like the seanchaí of old, to relate humorous, engaging stories and anecdotes in the rich, idiomatic Irish language.

Ó Grianna's stories have delighted both readers and language enthusiasts for decades. Here translated into English by the author himself, this collection of stories depicts the ordinary, innocently-portrayed Gaeltacht life – now virtually obliterated – and gives a fascinating insight into the unique life of late nineteenth and early twentieth century-speaking Donegal. They also convey the despair that his cherished dream of a Gaelic Ireland would never be realised.

Séamus Ó Grianna (1889-1969) was born and reared in Rannafast, Co. Donegal, one of the strongest bastions of the Gaelic language and its oral culture. He was embued with this rich, oral tradition which greatly informed and influenced his outlook and literary philosophy throughout his life.

MERCIER PRESS
WHAT YOU NEED TO READ

Islanders

Peadar O'Donnell

ISBN: 978 1 85635 472 1

A powerful novel of life in a small island community in Donegal, written by one of the Ireland's greatest historical and literary figures: socialist, republican, revolutionary and novelist, Peadar O'Donnell.

Peadar O'Donnell is a hugely important figure in Irish literature and Irish history, whose work should be on the shelves of every Irish reader and anyone interested in Irish culture.Islanders is a story of epic simplicity, of people who confront in their daily lives hunger, poverty and death.

'Islanders would be worth reading merely as a description of the lives of the poor on a wild, barren and beautiful coast, on which two bucketfuls of winkles may be a considerable addition to the wealth of the home … it is also a piece of heroic literature and as we read it we can positively rejoice in the heroism of human beings who can force a living from the rocks and live in charity with one another among the uncharitable stones' – Robert Lynd.

MERCIER PRESS
WHAT YOU NEED TO READ